"*You* sent me to jail."

Ferris's grip trembled on the gun pressed to Vance's forehead. Vance held one finger up out of Ferris's field of vision, a signal.

Panic flared in Stephanie. *Don't you dare try something reckless*, she mutely blazed at him.

Run, Vance mouthed to her.

The muscles in his arms bunched. He was going to make a move anyway.

She squeezed the trigger.

Her shot caught Ferris in the fleshy part of his shoulder. Vance scrambled up and bolted toward her.

"Away," she shouted to the dogs, praying Brutus would follow Chloe's lead. A rattle of semiautomatic fire sprayed the trees. Vance yanked her by the arm.

"Come on."

They sprinted down the path after the fleeing dogs. When they reached his vehicle, Vance flung open the rear passenger door and Steph and the dogs dove in. He did the same in the driver's seat, jammed the key in the ignition and gunned it.

Bullets fractured the rear window, glass ricocheting. She grabbed for the yelping dogs.

They'd have a precious head start, but not for long.

Dana Mentink is a nationally bestselling author. She has been honored to win two Carol Awards, a HOLT Medallion and an RT Reviewers' Choice Best Book Award. She's authored more than thirty novels to date for Love Inspired Suspense and Harlequin Heartwarming. Dana loves feedback from her readers. Contact her at danamentink.com.

Hunted on the Trail

DANA MENTINK

LOVE INSPIRED SUSPENSE

INSPIRATIONAL ROMANCE

LOVE INSPIRED® SUSPENSE
INSPIRATIONAL ROMANCE

ISBN-13: 978-1-335-48397-3

Hunted on the Trail

Love Inspired
22 Adelaide St. West, 41st Floor
Toronto, Ontario M5H 4E3, Canada
www.LoveInspired.com

Printed in U.S.A.

Repent ye therefore, and be converted, that your sins may be blotted out, when the times of refreshing shall come from the presence of the Lord. And he shall send Jesus Christ, which before was preached unto you: Whom the heaven must receive until the times of restitution of all things, which God hath spoken by the mouth of all his holy prophets since the world began.

—*Acts* 3:19–21

To Grandma Mentink, Junie the Wonder Dog
misses you, and we do, too.

ONE

"Bad idea. Very bad. The worst." Garrett, Stephanie Wolfe's twin, sounded much farther away than the three-hour drive to their family ranch house in Whisper Valley.

"You're wrong, it's a fabulous idea," she said firmly. "Finishing in the top three will net Security Hounds more cred." *Way more.* The four-day Lost Sierra Tracking and Trailing Competition would be yet another proving ground for Steph and her champion bloodhound, Chloe. From the back seat, Chloe flapped her ears in support of the idea.

"We're doing okay," he said.

"No, we're not." Their investigations firm took private cases and also did search and rescue for the county, and neither end had generated much activity of late. He knew it, she knew it and so did their other three siblings.

A windblown pine needle splattered against her SUV. The movement caught Chloe's attention and she slopped a giant tongue out the partially open window to capture it. Stephanie smiled at her canine passenger. Best dog she'd ever worked with, bar none. The purebred bloodhound, Duchess Chloe Cleopatra Rosamond, had been discarded by her breeders when she was discovered to have a flaw. In Steph's mind, her only flaw was her previous owners. "We won't get killed. Promise."

"Not funny."

"I leave funny to you, so put down the tennis ball and get going. I'll do the same."

He paused. "How do you know I'm fiddling with a tennis ball?"

"Please. I can tell you what you had for dinner."

"You can't."

"Cheese quesadillas with salsa and sour cream, no cilantro," she rattled off.

"I…" He stopped. "Well, there was no sour cream so I went without, for your information. Steph, I just feel uneasy about you tackling the Lost Sierra alone."

"You're gun-shy." He should be, after his last case. "And I'm not alone. I've got Chloe and the competition assigns you a partner." Because Garrett was right about one thing—the sprawling Northern California wilderness that spanned the Sierra Nevada crest was way too rugged and isolated to tackle solo, dog or no dog. Before he could rally a response, she brought out the big guns. "Catherine needs you to be with her when she testifies at the trial." An understatement, after his girlfriend had almost lost her entire family—and Garrett too—before they'd wrapped their last investigation.

He huffed. "Okay. I concede. I'll only be gone five days, tops. Roman and Chase…"

"Are away, leaving Mom, Kara and

Steph, the poor delicate females, to manage on their own."

"Don't kid. Weather's bad. The storm's gonna be a doozy."

The November forecast was grim. "Which will be an excellent test of Chloe's skills, and mine. Our cases don't always occur on lovely balmy days, right? It's only three nights."

He huffed. "The timing with Ferris's release…"

"Don't." She tried to smooth over her caustic tone. "I'm here. I'm doing this." *Read: I'm living my life and no one is going to stop me, especially not Ferris Grinder.*

His sigh was bone-deep, weary, which made her feel bad about adding to his worries.

"I got this, Garrett. Trust me."

"I do. Love you."

"Ditto."

She put away thoughts of Ferris and tackled the steep road up the mountain.

There was no sign of any human activity, only a wide sprawl of granite slope, heavily wooded. Had she taken a wrong turn?

Her brother's comment jangled. *The timing with Ferris's release...*

A memory crept in before she could shield against it.

The day in court, the trial for Maurice Grinder, Ferris's father.

Ferris had walked by on his way to the courtroom, passing where she stood in uniform. Chloe was there too. Her brother Chase had brought the dog as part of the ongoing training process, to accustom her to the sights and smells of a public building, and also, Steph suspected, as a show of moral support. Ferris stumbled and sent a chair flying at them, which clipped Chloe. Though there was no way to prove it, she knew Ferris had done it intentionally. Chloe reacted with a yelp and a spate of barking unlike she'd ever heard from her dog.

They'd convicted Ferris's father for his

fraudulent business practices, the fake trucking company that he used to steal freight and fence the goods. But there hadn't been enough evidence to get Maurice for what she believed deep down he'd also been responsible for: ordering the murders of an employee and his family after the clerk made plans to blow the whistle. Maurice had died in prison.

Ferris was shortly thereafter convicted of fraud, theft and assorted small crimes. If she'd been allowed to take on his case, maybe she could have gotten him for murder since she was sure he'd been the one to carry out his father's deadly contract. But Vance Silverton, her boyfriend at the time, who'd been promoted to detective instead of her, hadn't gotten the job done.

Steph eyed the roiling clouds as she drove deeper into the wilderness. Ferris had been paroled only three weeks earlier. There was no proof that he was behind the series of calls she'd received, anonymous promises that she and her dog would soon be dead. Former cops acquired lots of enemies, didn't they?

Teeth gritted, she drove on.

When she finally saw the tiny mile marker, she turned off toward a narrow bridge that spanned a river. To her relief, the metal security gate that barred access was unlocked and pushed aside, an indication she was heading the right way.

It was confirmed when she saw a short man with an orange vest on horseback. He waved her on. Abreast of him, she rolled down her window and he craned to look at her. His full beard almost covered the shiny ID tag on a pristine lanyard around his neck... Evan, volunteer.

"Here for the competition?" His gaze roved to her back seat. "Is that a liver-and-tan hound?"

"She is."

"A champion, huh?"

"Yes."

He laughed. "That's what they all say."

Rude. "With my dog it's the truth."

He pointed. "'Bout a half hour to go. I'll bring up the rear since you're the last pair."

Precisely thirty-five minutes later, they arrived at a small registration table, where a woman stood bundled against the cold, a banner with Lost Sierra Tracking and Trailing Competition snapping in the wind behind her.

Another woman sat nearby in a parked Jeep, poking at her phone.

Stephanie unloaded Chloe and approached the table. The registrar beamed her a smile from under the hood of her raincoat and they made their introductions.

"Excellent," Elizabeth said. "You're our last team. We've got your starts staggered, of course. Don't worry, winners are calculated strictly on elapsed time and course completion."

"How many teams are competing?"

"You're the tenth and final duo."

Perfect. She'd have a great shot at reaching the top three.

The woman pawed through a box under

the table and handed her a pack. "We've got six volunteers from the various tracking clubs to monitor the checkpoints. At the first checkpoint, you'll receive your tent and sleeping bag, as well as a GPS tracker. If you need to quit because of the storm at any time, have your partner radio and drive you back to your car. Your safety and your dog's is the first priority." She gestured as the woman in the Jeep got out. "Here she is. Her name is..." She sighed. "So sorry. I've forgotten. It's been a busy day."

The petite woman with a neat braid hastened over and pumped Steph's hand. "No problem. Gina Johnson. Pleased to meet you." She kneeled and scrubbed Chloe behind the ears, sending the dog's tail whipping. "You look like a winner to me, baby."

"She is," Steph said. "Many times over."

Gina grinned. "Well, let's go add another feather to her cap, shall we? I'll drive us to the starting point."

Volunteer Evan remained atop his horse, watching. "How about I escort you ladies to the first checkpoint?"

"No thanks," Gina said.

"Mighty rugged out there," Evan said. "Dangerous."

Gina waved him off. "I think we got this."

With a shrug, he dismounted and turned to help Elizabeth load supplies into her car.

Stephanie was about to follow Gina when she noticed a vehicle pull up and park under a tree. Her curiosity turned to shock as she watched a man get out. Tall, stubbled chin, and with a dimple on the right side of his mouth that would show if he'd been smiling.

He wasn't.

She couldn't make her brain believe he was standing there.

Not him.

Not now.

Vance Silverton realized his jaw was hanging open and closed it with a snap.

Steph? Here? That changed everything. His brain spun through the ramifications.

The woman with the braid who looked to be a volunteer strode to the Jeep and got in. Steph hadn't moved and was staring daggers at him. Stomach quivering, he freed the dog from the back seat to give himself a moment before he sauntered closer to Steph.

"Best behavior, Brutus," he muttered to the sluggish hound. "Hi, Steph." Friendly, casual. Maybe they could ignore the big fat white elephant of their past lazing between them. That notion immediately popped like a soap bubble.

"What are you doing here, Vance?"

"I was going to register."

"*You* were going to register? For this competition?" She eyed his dog incredulously. Brutus flicked one of his ears, the one that stood upright, before oozing like a puddle to the damp ground. Were a dog's legs supposed to spread out in all directions like that?

"You and him?" Steph looked as though she was not sure which point to tackle first. "Since when are you into tracking and trailing?"

Since never.

"I'm sorry, sir, but the competition is closed," the registrar called out. "We're not taking any more last-minute entrants because of the unfavorable weather forecast."

He was going to press his case, but there were other fish to fry now.

"Steph." He kept his voice low and took a step closer to her. "I need to talk to you. Privately."

A drop of rain landed on her short dark hair. She opened her mouth, closed it and then started in again. "No, you don't. I have no idea why you're here, but whatever it is, I don't want any part of it, or you."

Direct, like she'd been since they were colleagues. "Listen to me…"

"Elizabeth," Steph called over his shoulder to the woman in charge. "We're ready to roll."

Elizabeth finished shoving papers into boxes. She was too preoccupied to notice the awkward body language between him and Steph, but the other lady hadn't.

"Everything okay?" she called from the Jeep.

"Yes, one second, Gina," Steph said. "Let's go, Chloe."

He took her wrist. "Steph," he said urgently. "I really need to talk to you."

She jerked away from his touch. "I don't buy for one red-hot second that you're here to compete, so that means you're lying. I don't talk to liars."

He'd expected fireworks, but he thought he'd be able to at least explain before she shut him down. "Two minutes. It's important. I'm concerned about you."

"*Now* you're worried? That's real nice, Vance. You sure didn't spare many feelings about me when you took my job. Didn't care much then, did you?"

"I didn't…" He trailed off, snatching his baseball cap from his head and whacking the raindrops against his knee. But he had, actually. He'd done everything he could to get the detective promotion for reasons he couldn't tell her then. While he was trying to work out just what to say, she turned her back on him and trotted with her dog to the Jeep.

"Steph…" He'd taken a few steps when the registrar stopped him.

"Sir, this team has to get going before dark. Is there something else I can help you with?"

He eyed her box. "Aren't you going to stay until the event's over?" Three nights of sleeping under the stars, he'd read in the brochure. An eternity.

"Only until they reach the first checkpoint because they're the last team and the others are hours ahead. I'll wait in my car for their text and then go join the staff at the finish line camp site. We'll dispatch help from there if any is needed." She looked dubiously at Vance and his dog. "You're going to leave too, right? Storm's only getting started."

"Sure," he said faintly. "After one more pit stop for Brutus."

She arched an eyebrow at his lounging animal. "Um, don't be offended when I say this, but you might want to get your dog into better physical shape if he's going to compete."

Vance kept his expression neutral. "He's got a lot of inner-core strength."

To her credit, she did not laugh. "Okay." She loaded the carton under her arm into her vehicle along with the small table and climbed into her car.

Stephanie and Gina took off. The Jeep's headlights punched weakly into the gloom.

He rubbed a hand over his jaw. Maybe he was wrong. Maybe Ferris hadn't come to this pocket of nowhere and Vance had misread the clues he thought he'd found. But Stephanie Wolfe was here and that could not be dismissed as a coincidence.

He thought he'd been tracking Ferris. Now he had the sinking feeling he'd been played.

A spatter of rain hit his forehead. The isolation struck at him as he lost the distant sound of the Jeep. Just two women and a dog in a great big wilderness. He fingered his keys. Wouldn't hurt to add two more to the mix, and he probably had enough supplies to keep him and Pudge from starving for a while, just long enough to be sure she was safe. He could pretend to leave, then loop around and follow Steph and Gina without Elizabeth knowing. Steph would have a blowup of epic proportions if she found out he was trailing her.

But what she didn't know wouldn't hurt her.

He grinned down at Brutus. "All right, fella, it's time to follow our guts, and certainly you've got a lot of guts to follow."

The portly dog whipped his tail at him.

Whatever the fallout, he wasn't going to live with another failure. If he was wrong, he'd suffer the consequences. But if he was right…

He hoisted his dog into the car and cranked the ignition.

Gina drove slowly, keeping the Jeep in the center of the rugged trail, though the branches scraped the sides as they passed. Time was moving in painful slow motion.

Steph kept her chitchat light, to prevent thoughts of Vance from creeping in. The shock still shuddered through every bone and sinew, but she wasn't about to reveal that to her companion. "You got the short straw in escorting the last entrant?"

Gina shrugged. "Someone had to do it, so I offered. But I should get hazard pay, since everyone else got the benefit of a couple hours of daylight and no rain. This is going to be a once-in-a-lifetime experience. Great photos for my Instagram."

As they bumped on, Steph went over the map she'd been given. "Starting point should be coming up if you take this trail east."

"Got it." Gina peered into the gloom. "Man. It's only six o'clock but it might as well be night already."

She'd thought the same. She checked her own supplies and tested her flashlight again, then transferred the contents of the competition backpack to hers.

Gina shot her a surprised look. "You don't want the official gear?"

"I like my own stuff." Her supplies had saved her life once, and Chloe's too when the dog had been bitten by a snake while searching the heavy brush of a canyon. Her gear was personalized right down to the organic snacks she brought. It all came down to rule number two—your gear is the second most important thing for a successful search and rescue.

Gina shrugged. "Suit yourself but take this." She handed Steph a metallic pouch. "The contest sponsors provided it. Dog food. All organic or some such thing."

Steph took it to be polite, but she wasn't going to give Chloe any on account of rule number one—your dog is your most precious colleague. Chloe ate only what Steph had purchased or prepared with her own hands. She loved Chloe, had adored her since the moment her mom handed over the scrawny, underfed bloodhound who'd been dumped by the unscrupulous breeder in a shelter in Southern California. Five years ago, Chloe had been more ears than dog, but she'd grown and become a champion tracker and Steph's best friend. Sometimes she felt like her only friend, since Vance was no longer in her life. The miles stretched on, fifteen minutes bleeding into a half hour and beyond.

Stephanie rechecked the map and squinted through the rain-speckled windshield. "I wonder why I don't see any lights. Elizabeth said the checkpoint would be easy to spot. Oh, wait. There it is," Stephanie said. Off to their right, where the trail dipped down into a flat bowl of grassland and trees, shone a speck of white light.

"Whew. I was worried I'd gotten us lost." Gina drove them off the road and through a rutted path of grass. Stephanie held the door handle against the jostling, glad she'd tethered Chloe securely in the back seat. After a teeth-rattling twenty minutes, they arrived at the edge of a pine forest.

Stephanie let Chloe free and headed toward the light. "Hello," she called as they ducked under the trees. She'd expected to see a table, or at least a volunteer with a vest on, but there was no one, only a solitary lantern, beaded with moisture, hanging on a branch. Wind swirled the pine needles, speckling her with cold droplets. Goose bumps erupted on her skin. "I don't see a GPS tracker anywhere around, do you? Or the supplies?"

Gina frowned. "No. Maybe we did make a wrong turn and this isn't the spot. I'll grab my radio from the Jeep. Elizabeth is going to have to drive up here and help us out." She hurried off.

What was there to get wrong? They were supposed to receive their scent article, a sleeping bag and tent, and take a GPS tracker to carry along. Possibly they'd made an incorrect turn but why would there be a lantern hanging in some random place? Had there been a mix-up?

That probably explained it. She'd been a late entry and likely been left off a list or something. She texted Elizabeth with no response. Chloe was still sniffing, her sides gleaming in the twilight since it was now almost totally dark.

Stephanie looked closer. The lantern swung slightly in the breeze, sending the shadows crawling. Foreboding pulled at her stomach. No reason to jump to conclusions, she told herself. There was no threat here that she could detect. Chloe was calm and curious. She listened for the sound of Gina's return. Where was she? She would have had time to make it to the Jeep and back. Steph prickled with the desire to get out of the dark woods.

"Chloe." The dog immediately trotted to her side. She wanted to call out for Gina, but something made her stay silent as they hurried on. Branches cracked at the edge of the clearing.

They froze, listening. Chloe began to growl, nose quivering. Immediately, Steph pulled her weapon as they scurried back to the Jeep. Gina wasn't in the vehicle.

As she searched the ground for footprints, bullets erupted from a spot in the trees, spraying into the vehicle and carving chunks from the dirt. She grabbed her pack and yelled to Chloe, and they stumbled around to the other side. The shooting continued in a steady stream.

Semiautomatic, her brain told her. She cradled Chloe as the rear window glass showered down around them. Her ears rang with the torturous noise. The shots were sporadic, the noise growing closer.

The shooter was moving, closing the gap, coming to murder her. *Plan?*

She would not stand much of a chance at returning fire with any accuracy in the dark with the shooter firing at regular intervals. He'd edge around to get a better angle until his bullets penetrated the vehicle and cut them in half.

Her mouth and throat were dry with fear.

A noise behind her position spun her around.

An accomplice closing in from the rear? She fought down the bubbling panic as she clutched Chloe close.

All she could think of was how right her brother had been.

TWO

Vance's pulse hammered as he called over the rifle fire. "Steph, it's Vance."

"Vance?" she hissed.

"At your twelve, in the bushes. Stay low. Run to me when you can. I'll cover."

When he was sure she'd gotten onto her belly, he squeezed off cover fire, his shots peppering the trees and ringing across the valley at what he believed to be the gunman's position. The shooting stopped abruptly, but Vance continued until Steph and her dog tumbled into the bushes next to him. In the distance, he heard the firing of a motor, then the gunman flooring the pedal, moving rapidly away. *Coward.*

He breathed hard and lowered his weapon, wiping the sweat from his brow with a forearm.

Safe. For now. He offered a hand to help her up, but she ignored it. Before she could launch the inquisition, he went on the offensive. "Yes, I followed you. Yes, you can rip me to pieces later. But what's going on right now? Aside from the fun little shoot-out, I mean." He pointed over her shoulder to the Jeep.

She hesitated.

"Come on, Steph. Now is not the time to withhold." *Even from me.*

"There was no one at the checkpoint," she said. "No scent article or tracker. Gina went to get the radio out of the Jeep and now she's gone. No keys in the vehicle, but I didn't check closely because of the obvious."

Every sentence caused his stomach to cinch tighter. "Go get in my car. I'll check

the scene, make sure Gina's not hurt somewhere, and we'll clear out."

"I don't think so." Steph pulled a silver pouch of dog food from her pocket.
"Chloe and I will find Gina. Her scent is
on this."

He bit back a comment. Of course she
wasn't going to take the sensible option. It
was the stubborn, totally fearless attitude
that annoyed and attracted him in equal
measure. Maybe not completely equal, because at the moment she was stomping on
his last nerve. She offered the pouch to
the eager bloodhound pawing at her knee.

"Find." Her tone was calm, but he noted
her hand was trembling.

"This isn't safe," he said as she attached
a long lead to Chloe. She ignored him and
followed the tugging dog.

"It's Ferris," he called.

She stopped. Finally, she turned around.
"Explain that."

"I'm not gonna stand here and lay it all

out right now, but I know he's behind this. He's here. Close. Maybe he snatched Gina or shot her."

"You *know*?" Her mouth tightened, chin went up. "You're going to fill me in on how you came to that conclusion after I find Gina. She probably panicked and ran this way when the shooting started. Where's your dog? I can give him the scent too. Double-team it."

"Uh, he's in the car. He's a little…green."

Green and spectacularly unqualified. His new canine partner of two whole weeks, whom he'd recently renamed Brutus, likely hadn't located anything more significant than a dropped potato chip. Mercifully, Stephanie's dog tugged her away so all he could do was run after them, grateful he'd kept up the fitness regimen after leaving the force.

The dog beelined for the river that roared through a shrub-covered ravine. Vance gripped his own weapon as they sped along, taking up a flanking position while trying to avoid the branches clawing at his jeans. If the shooter—he knew down to his eyeteeth it was Ferris—was doubling back, they didn't have much time.

Stephanie plunged on, undaunted. The safest plan was to leave immediately, but if Gina was wounded…

Chloe stopped abruptly and he bumped Steph, catching her shoulder to keep from knocking her over. She jerked away as soon as she'd recovered her balance, shining a penlight from her pocket onto the ground. It took him a moment to spot it.

A footprint.

Steph didn't have to command her dog. Chloe had already resumed her search. He felt as if the forest had a million eyes, watching them. Hairs on the back of his neck tingled as he tried to track all the shadows and noises, which were soon swallowed up by the roar of rushing water.

They'd reached the edge of the riverbed. Stephanie stopped Chloe from charging over the lip of the rock and into the chasm. The dog whined.

He flicked on the flashlight he'd brought with him and angled it down into the water, the glow catching on the rocks and wild current. There was a narrow ribbon of earth paralleling the river, big enough for a motorbike or very small vehicle with a very confident driver.

"Did she double back maybe and we missed her?"

Steph shook her head. "Chloe would have tracked that." She looked again into the waves and he knew they were both thinking the same thing. If Gina had fallen in, she'd be no match for the current. Had she been shot?

New game plan. Steph was going to do the smart thing and lock herself in his car while he searched, whether she liked it or not, but the words died on his lips as he spotted the figure at the bottom.

"There she is," Steph said.

Her light was barely sufficient to catch

Gina's outline. The woman was lying on her side, holding on to a branch with both hands, resisting the pull of the water that threatened to snatch her.

He didn't wait for Stephanie's action plan. He holstered his gun, shoved his cell phone at her and plunged down the bank. Rock and dirt shifted, and he struggled to stay upright. "Hold on," he shouted over the waves. "I'm almost there." Her torso was being dragged by the flow, away from solid ground. As he neared, he detected the trembling in her arms.

"Almost there." He had to move faster but the ground near the bottom was mucky, suctioning his boots, and he fought for every step. The darkness concealed her face, but he caught the gleam of her profile as he approached.

He'd reached the water, extending to grab her wrists.

As he made contact, the whites of her eyes widened in the gloom.

And then she was gone.

He blinked in shock. He hadn't noticed her lose her grip, but she was whisked away, the feel of her wet sleeve lingering on his fingers.

No. He lurched a step forward. Steph shouted.

"Don't, Vance."

He wanted to ignore her, but she was right. He shouldn't leap into that violent water in the dark and leave Steph alone to fight Ferris. He stood peering into nothing, awash in fury and grief. If he'd moved faster, been stronger... She called again and he finally roused himself and scrambled back up the bank.

"I couldn't get her."

Steph touched his shoulder. She didn't say anything because she knew there was nothing to offer that would help. They'd navigated the cop life together, where people lived and died, and justice was a fleeting phenomenon. Knowing how to put aside the grief was the only way they could do their jobs. Gina would be added to the arsenal of memories he stored away in the dark places for the bleak moments when he could not keep them submerged.

"Steph, let's go to my car. Now." The urge to get her out of this place and call for help swamped him. Maybe Gina would be able to grab another branch downstream, haul herself out. A delusion, probably, but it helped for the moment.

Her expression was unreadable in the gloom. "Okay."

Limbs weary, he moved them to the edge of the trees, which provided some cover at least, and they hurried through the darkness. The moment they left the Lost Sierra, they could sort it through, talk to the police, figure out what happened. The "they" might be optimistic, but at least he'd make sure Steph was clear on every single detail before they parted ways again.

He led them to the spot where he'd parked the car in the trees that overlooked the meadow.

Steph pulled something from her pocket and groaned.

"What?"

"My satellite phone is broken. It was in my pocket when I dove for cover. I have my cell too, but no bars."

He checked his own. "Same." And he didn't have a sat phone.

He fisted his keys. "Exit plan. I'll turn around. The bridge is the quickest way out, and we might get some cell reception there when we pass the trees. Registration area's right there too. Elizabeth should be there still, and she's got a radio and sat phone, no doubt. We'll fill her in, then we all get out as fast as we can."

No argument from Steph. She opened the back door before he could get there and looked inside. "What's your dog's name?"

"Uh, Brutus," he said quickly.

"Move over, Brutus," she said. The dog wagged his tail, his bulk spread across the seat. He tilted his head at Chloe and quivered with excitement, but he didn't move.

"Over, Brutus. Scooch over," Vance ordered.

The dog wagged harder, his crooked tail whamming into the seat, his gaze riveted on the new arrival.

Vance hurried around, opened the other door and hauled his dog to the far side. Steph loaded Chloe, and the dogs gave each other a good sniffing before they settled in together.

"He's, you know, green, like I said."

"Uh-huh." She got into the passenger seat, poking at her phone. "Still no reception. I'll text Elizabeth, but I'm not sure it will go through. If she's left for some reason, the contest coordinators will realize something's wrong when they can't track the GPS we were supposed to be assigned."

But how long would that take?

"Texting Security Hounds too."

Security Hounds was her private-eye

business, he knew from his internet snooping. "Is there maybe a separate tracker in the gear they gave you?"

"No."

He focused on driving as fast as possible, which wasn't very fast at all considering the conditions. Wet, dark, cold. He felt her gaze riveted on him and he resisted the urge to squirm.

"Are you ready to tell me the truth?" she said.

He challenged, "Are you ready to listen?"

Waves of acid floated at him from the passenger seat. Fine. He had some feelings of his own. If she'd given him two minutes before she launched into this competition...

"My call to Elizabeth went through but she isn't answering."

"We'll get across the bridge and phone her again. If she doesn't answer, you can drive until you get a signal and I'll run back to the registration area and see if her car's still there."

"That's silly. Let's drive there together now. Check. Hit the bridge after."

But his instincts were hollering their loudest.

Get Steph out of here.

He swung to the left, having almost missed the turn.

"Vance." She didn't exactly clutch the door handle, but she looked like she was thinking about it. Back-seat driver, always had been. They'd constantly battled about who would drive whenever they'd had to travel together as cops.

She'd accused him of driving like a sixteen-year-old who was afraid of scratching his father's Buick. He said her recklessness made him feel like he was a passenger in a getaway car. He almost smiled as the steep slope to the bridge came into view. Steph held on as he made the perilous descent. He was about to launch into the explanation of his presence when he braked hard.

"What...?" Steph's question trailed off.

They both got out to take a closer look.

His headlights caught the gleaming metal gate, which was now stretched across the bridge and secured with a padlock. They were sealed off from exiting, this way at least.

Stephanie blew out a breath. "Maybe Elizabeth left, locked it to prevent any more last-minute arrivals on her way out."

"I don't think so."

Shoulder-to-shoulder, they stood in silent thought.

Someone wanted them trapped here, cut off and vulnerable.

And he knew exactly who that someone was.

Steph chewed her lip. Vance no doubt had the same thought she did. *Ambush.* "Back to the registration area. My car's there and there's an old satellite phone in the back we can power up. Hopefully Elizabeth will be there safe, too. We have to warn her the bridge is locked and there's a shooter."

Vance juggled the wheel. "She had to have wondered why you haven't checked in yet. She might have called it in already."

She ripped open the map again, shining her penlight on the paper as he spun the wheel in a tight arc and floored it. "If Elizabeth has left, our next best exit option is north of here. A road that cuts through the valley. It'll eventually take us to the highway."

"Copy that," he said.

The phrase was so natural and yet so much a part of their shared past that it stabbed her like an ice pick. She didn't like the pain. Anger was better. She clenched the map. "Start talking."

"Oh, *now* you want me to talk?" His nostrils flared, his biceps flexing as he detoured around a mudhole. "We could have avoided this if you'd listened to my talking earlier."

She goggled at his audacity. This was her fault? "You blame me for not wanting to chit chat with you, Vance?"

He rolled his eyes. "It wouldn't have killed you to listen for two minutes. I told you it was urgent and you should have believed me. I guess now you do, huh?"

She couldn't see his eyes spark green fire, but she knew that's what she would have noted, light permitting. He had a point, unfortunately. Her emotions at seeing him had overridden her good sense, and anger wasn't going to get them out of whatever jam they were in. She took a breath. "Vance," she said calmly as they hurtled along, chasing the last flicker of gray in the blackening sky. "Give me a sitrep. Please."

Her attempt at control worked. His wide shoulders resettled. The fringe of his crew cut brushed the roof of the car and the wheel looked like a toy in his hands. Why had such a big man chosen such a small vehicle? Vance was always the tallest in the room, a full eight inches above her, which made her head tuck nicely under his chin when they'd hugged during their six months of friendship that had turned to romance. *Focus, Steph.*

"Short story is, I took early retirement after Ferris was locked up. I'm a bounty hunter now. Have been for a year or so."

Fortunately, the gloom covered her look of surprise. "Okay." She desperately wanted to know why he'd quit the force, especially after betraying her to steal her job, but it was more important to get the facts. "And you're tracking Ferris because..."

"He skipped out on his probation officer three weeks ago, but I've been sticking my nose into his business since the day I quit the force."

"Why?"

He snagged a look at her. "Because he's a killer who never got what he deserved."

A killer whom they believed helped his father execute his clerk and family. She suppressed a shiver. Without sufficient evidence to try Ferris for murder, the department had settled for what they could get like they had for his father, Maurice. Settling was never her go-to. Vance's either.

Vance's skull thunked the roof as they bounced over a rough spot. "We missed something. *I* missed something and Ferris got away with murder. I decided I'd use my bounty-hunter status to keep him on my radar while I searched for more info, some witness that overheard Maurice and Ferris planning the murders, an inmate who might have caught a comment from Maurice before he died in jail. I'd feed whatever I uncovered to the cops. When Ferris ditched his parole officer, I had legal permission to go after him. At least I could send him back to jail for *that* minor offense while I kept digging."

Surprising. She'd assumed Ferris was one of those losses they'd both had to swallow whether they liked it or not. "How'd you track him here?"

"I followed him to the Shasta Cascade region, then the Lost Sierra specifically. A couple weeks back I found some brochures he'd looked at about the competition in a hotel room he'd vacated. He's a slob, by the way. Left trash everywhere and not even a tip for the housekeeper. My aunt Lettie would have been disgusted. The brochures were about this tracking-and-trailing competition. Made no sense that a man like him would be interested. I tried to do my undercover thing—enter, to poke around—but I was too late. Then I…saw you."

His voice throbbed when he said it. *Saw you.* He'd certainly awakened a reaction in her too, but she wasn't about to admit that.

Vance let out a huge breath. "Steph, at first I thought Ferris skipped out on parole and I was tracking him until I realized you were here. Now I think he knew I was following him and he left the clues for me to find. Ferris wanted us both here at the same time. I think he's trying to make us pay."

"Us? Why me? It wasn't even my case when Ferris was convicted. It was yours." The words were hard, like river stones.

"Yeah, Ferris was mine, but you got it started and you helped the detective seal the deal on his dad. Maurice went to jail kicking and screaming and died there. My new theory is Ferris blames us for that and he's going to even the score. Maurice's life for yours and mine."

She considered the comment Maurice Grinder had flung at her at the sentencing. *You crossed the wrong family.* It had been followed by a string of expletives fired directly at her before he was removed from the courtroom. She suppressed a shiver. "So you think he's lured us both here because he's got some plot cooking to kill us? Why now? Why risk his freedom when he was legally released?"

For a moment there was only the sound

of the rain driving against the window. His gaze drifted to hers. "Know what date it is?"

"November fifteenth. What does that…?" Her words died away. The year before on November 15th Maurice Grinder had died in prison, where she'd put him. Her throat went dry.

He turned up the wiper speed to match the increasing rain.

"Walk me through it. How did you land at this event, Steph?"

"I got an email last week, telling me there was an unexpected opening because a team dropped out."

"From whom?"

"A generic Gmail account. The message included basic info and a phone number."

"And?"

"And I called, and I entered."

"Anything out of the ordinary about that process?"

"No…" She reconsidered. "Actually, I did think the registrar, Elizabeth, seemed surprised. She asked me how I'd heard about it and she said she didn't know their publicity person had reached out personally to anyone, nor was she aware of a team dropping out. They were happy to have me and she handled the application, even after the deadline had passed."

"Likely it wasn't their publicity person who contacted you. Easy to create a fake email account."

"But to lure me into a contest to kill me? Us? Drop clues for you to follow here? It would be a lot of work for Ferris. Kind of an elaborate plan. Why not just take us out in Whisper Valley someday? I'm regularly out with Chloe on some trail or another and you're fishing all the time. A quick shot and we're dead."

"I'm not fishing all the time, but never mind that. He chose here because he's not going to have witnesses, or any trouble getting in and out unnoticed. What better place to do it, Steph? On the anniversary of the day his father passed away?"

Hundreds of acres of wilderness. No communication. A hard knot began to form in her belly.

"He'd have to assume I had a sat phone. No way for him to predict it was out of commission. I could simply call for help."

"Unless he figured you'd be dead before you could do that. He'd planned to end it at the first checkpoint. Kill me too, maybe, along the road in or out."

Vance could be wrong. She didn't want to believe it, that she'd fallen so easily for Ferris's lies. If it was Ferris, she'd been blindsided and her unwillingness to listen had delivered her squarely under his control. She wasn't going to share that little kernel with Vance.

Ruthless, that was exactly how she'd describe the Grinder family. Lawrence Harlow, the man who ran one of Grinder's warehouses, realized Grinder was maintaining a fictitious trucking company from which he'd dispatch various criminals to steal freight he then resold.

Harlow had been prepared to go to the police. Another employee named Jack tipped off Grinder and the Harlow family—four people—was dead within hours, gunned down by an assassin that was never caught.

Steph believed Ferris had pulled the trigger on the Harlows himself, but there was no physical evidence to prove it. For some unaccountable reason, Lawrence Harlow had opened the door for his killer. She'd never been able to figure out why.

Maybe if Vance hadn't wanted to stroke his own ego by taking the detective's job...

Let it go. You're happy to be rid of police work, remember?

That much was true. Mostly. God was growing her up in a new direction, as her mother often reminded her. And she'd been glad to be clear of Vance too, until he landed in her sphere again like a meteor falling from the sky.

"When's the official finish to this competition?"

"Saturday evening." And it was only Wednesday.

Brutus whined from the back seat.

"Can you turn on the radio?" Vance said. "The country station? Brutus gets nervous when he's riding and then he throws up, but music seems to help."

"This doesn't seem like a good time for music."

"It's not a good time for upchucking either and he ate a bag of cheese puffs I had stashed in my hotel room so that's not gonna be pretty."

"Are you kidding?"

"Dead serious."

She shook her head. "You were never dead serious."

"I was. A lot."

"Like you were the first week I transferred into the department?" He'd snuck into her assigned car and set the emergency lights, siren, radio, wipers, air-conditioning controls, signals and anything else he could find to turn on when she started the engine. She'd finally gotten it all deactivated and found the other three members of her shift laughing at her. She'd laughed too because teasing meant you were part of the brotherhood…even if you were a sister. Vance had always been able to make her laugh like no one else. And cry.

"Got your attention, right?"

"It did.

"It was a little welcome-to-the-force gesture."

And his wide smile and deep baritone laugh had sparked a connection between them that had grown deeper and wider, like water funneling to the sea. They'd dated only when they were in separate supervisory chains, on and off, two and a half years before. Vance, in fact, worked a graveyard shift and their time together was stolen moments that seemed all the sweeter for it. They'd started in on that relationship that lasted six lovely months until the Harlow family was murdered.

After that, her work to convict Maurice became so engrossing she'd not noticed them begin to edge apart. Vance turned his focus on Ferris and his desire to put him away was all he ever talked about.

They'd both been consumed. She'd assisted the lead detective to convict Maurice while a preliminary case was being assembled against Ferris. She knew they'd get Ferris too and it was part of what she looked forward to when she'd applied for the detective slot. Vance said she'd be great. And then he'd also applied and let spill personal details about her that blew up her chances. His betrayal hurt like nothing else she'd ever experienced, and she'd left the force.

Thunder sounded in the distance and Brutus howled.

"The radio," Vance insisted. "Or he's gonna hurl and I just got the back seat clean."

Steph fiddled with the knobs, glancing at the dogs. Chloe had scooted over, draping her head over the shivering Brutus. "Good girl, Chloe." She noted Brutus's ample belly oozing out from under Chloe's muscular frame. If that dog was a trained tracker, she was the Queen of England.

"I'm gonna need some backstory on Brutus."

Her cell phone pinged.

"Saved by the bell," Vance muttered as a fork of lightning split the sky.

THREE

Steph peered at the phone and pumped her fist. "We must be able to get a connection here. It's a text from Elizabeth." She let out a cheer. "'Team located volunteer, Gina, injured but alive. Transported to hospital. Holding at registration area until you get here.'"

He felt a ponderous weight lifted from his heart and he breathed a silent thanks to the Lord that Gina had survived. He was going to make sure all four of them did too. Now that task would be a ton easier with help on the way.

Steph's fingers flew and she dictated her own follow-up message. "'Are you advised shooter at large in vicinity?'" After a moment Elizabeth replied and Steph sighed. "She said affirmative. Police dispatched. Gina must have told her."

They both flopped back on the seats, buoyed by the knowledge that they were no longer cut off. Rescue was imminent. All they had to do was wait with Elizabeth. Between them they had enough firepower to fend off the shooter if he showed up again.

Police on the way. Gina found. He tried to assemble the sequence in his mind as he guided the car toward the registration area. Had Gina been spotted and rescued by a competitor? Unlikely, since the other parties were several hours ahead. New scenario. She'd crawled out of the water on her own and contacted Elizabeth…how? There was limited connectivity in the area and whatever phone Gina had been carrying had been inundated when she fell in the river. Could have been in a waterproof case, he supposed.

Steph was still tapping keys. "Ugh. Lost

the signal again before I could send the text to Security Hounds."

They drove in silence for a few minutes. He looked over to find her drumming her fingers on the knee of her jeans. Finger tapping. A tell he'd seen before.

"You're tapping."

"And you're tugging your earlobe."

He realized he was doing exactly that. She wasn't the only one with a tell. His honorary Aunt Lettie would have noticed it too and teased him about it. "I'm giving the situation the sniff test."

"Me too."

"And it smells funny."

"Uh-huh."

"Last I saw Gina she was being swept downstream, away from the competition course."

"Elapsed time?"

He checked his watch. "That was probably two hours ago by my calculation, maybe a little more."

"Two hours," she repeated.

"So Elizabeth's team had time to locate Gina, get her out, move her by vehicle to a hospital before Elizabeth contacted us?"

"Could be they had a medical vehicle standing by."

"Uh-huh." No choice but to say it. "It's also possible that Elizabeth and Ferris are partners. He might have threatened or bribed her into cooperating."

Steph continued to tap. "Or it's not her we're messaging." She stared for a moment. "I'm thinking about my days in the academy. I had a training captain who used to drum into me 'by failing to prepare we're preparing to fail.'"

"Yep."

"All right," she said slowly. "If it's actually Ferris or his accomplice who we're driving to meet, how about we have a little surprise ready for him?"

"My thoughts exactly." He couldn't stop the slow smile that spread over his face and the tickle in his stomach at her grit. She was tough and he'd been enchanted by it and by her, once upon a time. They'd dated in fits and starts, but he was always drawn back to her, no matter the tug of their careers. Toward the end of their months of casual dating he'd started to fall in love with her until he'd thrown it all away. Not the moment to wade through that again, but he could admire her, couldn't he? Nothing wrong with that. They had a plan together in under a minute, stopping a quarter mile from the staging area where the whole debacle had begun.

Brutus was reluctant to leave the car, but when Chloe exited, he decided to follow. They led the dogs to a deeply shadowed pocket near a tower of rock, overlooking the staging area.

"Elizabeth's car's there, parked under a tree near yours."

Even with their night-vision binoculars, they could not make out if anyone was behind the wheel. Dogs in tow, they took a slow route through the trees, creeping closer. Elizabeth's car was still and dark under the trees, while Steph's vehicle was fifty feet away.

"Will Brutus maintain a silent stay?" she whispered as they stopped at a thick cluster of shrubs that separated them from Elizabeth's parking place.

"Yes," his mouth said. *We'll find out*, his brain corrected. "If Ferris shows up, I'll initiate contact."

She looked as though she was going to argue, but instead she nodded. "I'll cover."

Brutus whined.

"It's okay, boy," he whispered. "Sit. Stay." That sounded more or less how Stephanie and her siblings would command their dogs.

The dog's whine turned into a yip.

"Quiet," he admonished as loud as he dared.

Chloe looked at her compatriot and slathered a tongue over his snout. The dog quieted for a moment, but then with a pitiful cry he hauled himself up and dashed away into the bushes.

"Brutus," Vance called. Great. Now was the worst moment possible for the animal to show an independent streak. The dog was plenty slow so Vance only had to jog between the shrubs, but he got slashed in the face by wet branches for his effort. He was moving too quickly to adjust when he came upon Brutus standing like a stone, and he somersaulted over the top of him, landing on his face in the wet pine needles at the edge of the clearing, not five feet from Elizabeth's car.

Steph appeared with Chloe. "What is going on?" she whispered. "Is this your idea of stealth?"

He got up and froze as he saw the heel of a boot protruding from under the shrubbery.

He gave Steph a hand signal and she immediately stopped in her tracks.

Chloe did too. Through the branches, he could see both cars, quiet, beaded with raindrops. He drew his gun and skirted around Brutus, who was shaking and whining, attention fixed on the boot.

The dripping shrubs covered the person wearing the boot. Brutus whimpered softly as Vance pressed closer. Maintaining cover until the last minute, he kicked the branches away.

Elizabeth was lying on her back, eyes staring, the dark spot of a bullet hole gleaming in the center of her forehead.

He reached down and checked for a pulse. He knew he wouldn't find one. Elizabeth was dead. Before or after he locked the bridge, Ferris had probably wormed his way into her car somehow while she waited for Steph to check in, killed her, then used her phone to text them, or something else along those lines. He might be getting a bead from a hidey-hole right now, ready to shoot them.

"Steph…" He stopped talking at the sound of movement right behind him.

* * *

Steph gripped her weapon, palms slick. Chloe barked savagely. She'd thought they had the upper hand, since there were two of them, but the tables had turned in a moment.

Neither of them had reacted quickly enough before Ferris charged out from behind a tree.

Before either could get off a shot, Ferris had the pistol to Vance's temple. He swiveled to face Steph, using Vance's body for cover.

Chloe kept on barking.

"Shut that dog up," Ferris snarled.

"Chloe, silent." The dog settled into plaintive whines, which were echoed by Brutus. Steph clenched her gun and sized up her options, adrenaline igniting her nerves. "Drop it, Ferris."

"Sure. Let me just do that right now, Officer Wolfe." His voice was exactly as she remembered—high-pitched, nasal. "Anything to accommodate."

The watery moonlight left him in shadow, but she saw with a jolt that he was wearing a Kevlar vest. Vance was right. Ferris had been plotting. Her bullets wouldn't make a dent, not where he was shielded anyway.

He'd come prepared. *Failing to prepare meant preparing to fail.* She hadn't prepared and her own gullibility sickened her. Would Vance die because of her failure? Would she and the dogs be killed too?

Vance was a tense silhouette, his gun still gripped in his raised palm. Maybe they had a chance if they could distract Ferris.

But Ferris pressed his gun hard into Vance's temple and stripped Vance's revolver loose with the other hand, tucking it in his waistband. She resisted the fear that crept along her spine. Vance was unarmed, nothing between him and a bullet to his brain except her.

She mulled over the options as Chloe stood quivering at her side. The dog wanted a command, something to tell her what to do, but Chloe was not an attack dog and Steph could only tell her "steady," which hopefully would keep her from jumping into the line of fire. Brutus cowered on the path, alternately trembling and growling in terrified uncertainty.

Vance locked gazes with her as he talked to Ferris. "You left an easy trail. It was a piece of cake to follow you. What happened to the great criminal mastermind?"

Ferris laughed. "That's a cop thing. You always believe you're the smartest people in the room. What arrogance," he said, emphasizing the point by smacking the gun into Vance's brow. "That's the thing I can't stand about cops."

"It's not arrogance. We really are smarter than you," Vance said through gritted teeth.

Why was Vance goading the man who had a gun to his head?

"So smart you let me lead you right here so I can kill you both," Ferris said. "Geniuses, you two." He held up a bunch of red wires. "Your spark-plug wires, Officer Wolfe. Disabled your vehicle just in case you made it back to your car before I was ready." He tucked them in his pocket.

"Put down the weapon, Ferris," Steph commanded before Vance could antagonize him any further. "Cops are coming. You have no way out."

He rolled his eyes, pale glimmers in the darkness. "Do they have a class in cop school to teach you how to lie? I always wondered that. There's no one coming. You know it, Officer Wolfe, and so do I."

"The contest coordinators will miss us when we don't check in."

He laughed, a hearty guffaw. "You don't get it, do you? I'm checking in as Elizabeth using her phone. Already alerted the officials that you and Gina decided to back out due to the storm and you've left the area. For good measure, I told them you'd decided to check into a hotel to wait out the storm. If your family calls to check on you, that's what they'll be told. No one will know that anything's wrong. By the time they do, it'll be too late."

Too late. The words chilled her.

He tapped the gun against Vance's cheekbone. "Now that I think about it, maybe I am a criminal mastermind."

Steph eased an inch to her left, desperate for a clear shot that wouldn't kill Vance. "All this. Just to punish me? Because I put your father in prison?"

"Originally, to punish you, yes, but when Officer Vance here decided to follow me, I figured two birds, one stone, right?"

"You were a free man," she said. "You served your sentence and you're throwing that all away because you're upset that you and your dad got caught for breaking the law?"

"And why would I be upset about that, Officer Wolfe? Because you harassed my family? It was humiliating for all of us. We couldn't show our faces anywhere. My favorite cousin had to move out of town to avoid the shame of it."

Vance smiled. "'Whatever is begun in anger, ends in shame.' That's a Ben Franklin quote. I read it on a cereal box. You should read more, Ferris. It would do you good."

Shut up, Vance, she wanted to shout at him. "Your father got what he deserved."

"You forced my father to spend his last days in prison, where he *died*. Sharing a cell and a toilet in a six-by-eight-foot space with cement walls. And *you* sent me to jail so I couldn't even visit him before he passed." His grip trembled on the gun as he pressed it to Vance's brow. "Nothing upsetting about that?" he spat, the saliva spraying out at her. "Maybe you'd understand better if it was your family. All those precious brothers and sisters, your sweet mommy."

With effort, she let the comment deflect off her. Another half inch and she could risk it. She leaned as slowly as she could.

"Cops are all alike," Ferris said. His grip tightened on the trigger and a vein in Vance's jaw jumped. He held one finger up out of Ferris's field of vision, a signal.

Panic flared in her. This was a lose-lose scenario. This close, people would die— Vance first. *Don't you dare try something reckless*, she mutely blazed at him.

Run, Van mouthed to her.

The muscles in his arms bunched. He was going to make a move anyway.

She squeezed the trigger.

Her shot caught Ferris in the fleshy part of his shoulder, less than an inch from the Kevlar covering. He spun back with a grunt. Vance scrambled away and bolted toward her.

"Away," she shouted to the dogs, praying Brutus would follow Chloe's lead. She squeezed off some shots, which sent Ferris retreating behind Elizabeth's vehicle. While she was deciding whether she had enough of an advantage to outgun him, a rattle of semiautomatic fire sprayed the trees as Ferris appeared over the hood. Vance yanked her by the arm.

"Come on."

They sprinted down the path after the fleeing dogs. When they reached his vehicle, Vance flung open the rear passenger door and Steph and the dogs dove in. He did the same in the driver's seat, then jammed the key in the ignition and gunned the engine.

Bullets fractured the rear window, glass ricocheting. She grabbed for the yelping dogs.

"Stay down," Vance yelled.

Unnecessary. She was flat on her stomach, one arm around Chloe and the other anchoring Brutus. Ferris's next round of bullets would have cut Vance down if he hadn't floored the gas, getting them far enough away that the shots sheared off the side mirror and punched into the doors.

With them out of range, Ferris would have to return to Elizabeth's vehicle or Steph's, or perhaps he had another stashed somewhere. They'd have a precious head start, but not for long. She quickly checked the dogs.

Vance's anxious gaze caught hers. "You hurt? The dogs?"

"We're okay, except Brutus looks a little green around the gills."

Vance flipped on the country music and the dog immediately relaxed.

Steph gaped. If they hadn't almost been murdered not two minutes before, the situation would have been positively comical. Running for their lives with a carsick dog and someone singing about a pickup truck and a high-school sweetheart.

She grabbed a blanket and brushed the glass off the seat, covering the sharp bits with the floor mats to protect the dogs' paws. Then she squirmed her way into the front.

Vance was heading for the bridge, which would have been the quickest exit if it wasn't locked up. They'd have to try ramming through. A bruise was rapidly forming on his brow and blood trickled from a cut that flowed into his eyes. She pulled a piece of gauze from her pack and pressed it to his wound. "Hold this."

He did with one hand, shooting her an incredulous glance. "I can't believe you took that shot."

"Really?" She taped the gauze in place. "You can't?"

He blinked at her. "Actually, I can believe you took it, even though my skull was in the vicinity."

"I'm a crack shot."

"Fortunate for me, but it wasn't necessary. I was working on a diversion."

"Saved you the trouble." Her words were cool, but her stomach muscles quivered.

Truthfully, she didn't want to consider what the negative consequences of her actions might have been. A hair to the right and… She'd known, somehow, that God wouldn't let her fail in that moment, wouldn't let Vance suffer at her hand. Was it simple hubris or faith talking? She wasn't sure, and not being sure was uncomfortable.

She returned the gauze and tape back to her pack.

He continued to ride the gas. "We're outgunned unless you have a rifle in your backpack."

"Negative."

"Elizabeth's car isn't a four-by-four. Mine's better for off-roading so that's an advantage, at least."

"Uh-huh." She narrowly avoided smacking her head on the side as he pivoted around a boulder in the road.

"He's probably not far behind us. Lots of spots near the bridge where he could pick us off." The blood had begun to seep through the gauze. He looked at her. "Run or hide, Steph?"

Everything relied on their decision. Sweat pricked her forehead. "I need to think."

"Think fast."

It annoyed her to be pressed, especially

by him, but the seconds were flying away like birds startled from a nest. "I say run. Ram our way through the bridge gate, get high enough that we can snag a signal. Do you agree?"

Vance maneuvered around a fallen tree, eyes flicking to the rearview. "I say we hide. Let him pass us. Double back to the bridge and see if we can spring the lock. I have a trick for doing that."

"Dodgy."

"Yes. Pluses and minuses." He held up a fist. "Rock, paper, scissors?"

Was he serious? "You know I can't stand that when you throw it all to chance instead of—"

"Making lists? Calculating outcomes? Convening committees? Steph, we've got about five minutes tops before he's on our tail. There's no time for a spreadsheet on this one."

"I don't make spreadsheets," she snapped.

"Yeah, I remember when you enacted your coffee-room campaign. You'd been there less than a week before you created an Excel spreadsheet and had us all slotted in to man the supplies and tend to the coffeepot."

"That needed to be done. Half the time there was no coffee and everyone was in a panic when there wasn't time to Door-Dash Starbucks."

"True story. Never was an upset coffee drinker after that. But you gotta go with your gut here. Stop overthinking."

She bridled at his tone, but they'd come to the steep descent that would ultimately end at the bridge. He pulled the car deep into the shadowy shoulder and reached for his belt.

"Where are you going?"

"Recon. Keep the dogs quiet."

"Vance," she snapped, but he'd already headed for the rock, crouched low with the night-vision binoculars pulled from his pack.

Her mouth was open to retort. Both

dogs looked at her expectantly from the back seat, eyes wide and trusting in the darkness.

Was delaying the best plan? She had no idea, but she wasn't going to sit idly in the car and wait for the big, strong man to figure out their next move.

"Stay," she said quietly. Chloe sat obediently, but Brutus looked as though he might howl. She fished a couple of sticks of jerky from her pack and presented one to each dog. Brutus sniffed cheerfully and gently took the offered treat. At least he had good manners.

She snuck out and joined Vance where he was crouched, peering down at the road. No need to ask any questions. She hunkered next to him and waited in silence, ticking off the seconds in her mind.

The crunch of rock under tires sent her pulse spiraling.

Elizabeth's car rolled past their hiding place, Ferris in the driver's seat, his head swiveling back and forth. He might be able to track where they'd left the road but she didn't think so. The ground was rocky enough to resist tire prints and she grudgingly admitted that Vance had chosen the perfect spot to leave the trail. Ferris drove toward the bridge, stopped, waited, then reversed his direction and rolled onward until he was obscured by trees.

She heard Vance exhale. "We'll give him four minutes and then beat it to the bridge. Okay?"

"Vance, you're obviously going to do whatever you want. Don't bother asking for my opinion."

He chuckled softly. "It gets your goat when I'm right, doesn't it?"

She wanted to smack him in the shoulder. "Even a broken clock—"

"Is right twice a day," he said, finishing her thought. "Quick. Time for your part of the plan. Let's go before I'm wrong again, huh?"

There was no choice but to hurry after him and pray they got to the bridge before Ferris found them.

FOUR

Steph's legs ached from bracing them against the floorboards. Vance had to keep the car to a crawl since he didn't dare turn on the headlights. The wind had risen to a howl, which would help smother any sound of their progress, and the undulating canopy of branches overhead couldn't hurt either. She prayed Ferris had continued in the direction they'd seen him take. So far there was no indication he had an accomplice.

The wheels spun in the mud for a heart-stopping moment until they broke free. To minimize the risk of being spotted, Vance was driving on a trail that wasn't meant for vehicles, that much was clear. At one point the path narrowed so severely, with drop-offs on either side, that she had to get out her flashlight and direct his progress.

As he navigated the descent, Steph held on to the doorframe, wishing she'd taken the time to tether the dogs. They slid and scrambled as they tried to stay on the seat. At the bottom, she could see it now—the gate secured by the shiny new padlock.

Bolt cutters. What she wouldn't give for a pair. Normally she'd carry a small version if she was going on an extended search with Chloe. No telling where she might encounter a livestock fence to keep trespassers out. Trespassing was never her preference, but if Chloe indicated there was a lost child or confused senior on the other side of the fence, she'd cut locks first and ask for forgiveness later. Why hadn't she brought cutters along?

Because you were bamboozled into thinking this was a competition. "Bamboozled" was a word her father would have used. *Too gentle, Dad*, she thought.

"Duped" sounded more like it and she'd not suspected a thing.

The ease with which Ferris had tricked her caused her stomach to churn. If she'd listened to Vance… That brought the churning to a whole new level, which was only going to make things more difficult. *Fix the immediate problem, Steph.* Shooting out the lock might draw Ferris's attention if he wasn't too far away. She finally realized Vance was trying to get her attention.

"Under your seat." He pointed. "Toolbox."

She grabbed it out. "You have bolt cutters in here? Why didn't you say so?"

"Not bolt cutters, my second gun. Take it. You'll need two rocks to deal with the padlock, but there are plenty around to choose from." He stopped her question with a quick look. "It's a cheap padlock. You whack both sides with the rocks at the same time and it'll pop open." He pantomimed how with his palms and the gear-shift.

She lifted her brow. "How'd you learn that trick?"

"Retired United States Marine, remember?" He wriggled his eyebrows. "We do things, and we know stuff."

She didn't argue with that. Vance did seem to know about an endless variety of topics from how to restring guitars to the best way to boil an egg. It had been a constant source of amusement to their police squad, and to her.

"Why didn't we do that earlier when we first found the bridge locked?"

"Because, if you recall, we thought it was a trap and we were going to be picked off like ticks on a coonhound."

"We might be anyway."

"The difference is now we have no choice."

No choice. Just the way Ferris wanted it.

He drove the last steep yards to the bridge, put the vehicle in Park and yanked the emergency brake. He left the engine running but the lights off. "Gonna find a high point and recon while you're at the bridge. Texting's probably still spotty. Whistle if you can't handle the lock."

She bristled. "I'll handle it, one way or the other."

"Well then, whistle when you clear it. Dogs in or out?"

"Chloe can stay in with the window down in case I need to give her a command."

He lowered the rear window while she collected her pack. In case his rock trick didn't work, she was going to try dismantling the gate hinge and she'd brought a few small tools of her own from her backpack. It'd take far too long if she had to go at it with her meager equipment, but desperate times...

Brutus yipped and they both yanked a look at him.

"I'm doubtful your dog can stay quiet if he's not snacking," Steph grumbled.

"You wound us with such aspersions." The comment was glib, but Vance actually sounded a bit offended.

Brutus was already starting to dance anxiously from paw to paw. It wouldn't do to have him baying in panic. That sound would carry for miles.

"He's quiet when he's close to me and I can keep my hands free," Vance said. "I'll sling him along."

She blinked. "You'll do what now?"

He rolled his eyes. "I know it sounds weird, but I got one of those baby slings for him because he gets tired and he's too awkward to carry on my back."

"A…baby sling?"

Vance ignored her astonishment and grabbed a blue cloth sling from the between-seats compartment. The material was cloud patterned. He threaded Brutus inside. The dog's gangly legs overlapped the edges and he seemed deliriously happy to be so close to Vance. Such a load would be ungainly for a smaller man, but Vance seemed unfazed.

"This gets weirder and weirder," she muttered.

"Cut the chatter and move out, Wolfe." With a roguish wink, he turned his back on her and strode toward the rocks.

"Be right back, Chloe." The dog's droopy gaze riveted to Steph as she got out and found a couple of rocks before she hurried to the bridge. "All right. Wonder if this trick will actually work." The first whack of the rocks accomplished nothing except that she banged her knuckles.

"Owww."

The second blow seemed to loosen the lock, or maybe it was wishful thinking.

The third hit sprung the locking mechanism loose. Her mouth fell open. Incredible. The rock thing really did work. She felt like pumping her fist but instead she pocketed the padlock and opened the gate. She shoved it wide, the metal squealing. Combining with Chloe's bark, the sound carried in the thin air. Chloe's bark turned to a howl.

The dog was standing on the back seat, head shoved out, yowling for all she was worth. Reacting to the shriek of the gate? Signaling danger? From where?

She pulled her weapon and did a 360.

From somewhere up slope she heard the sound of crackling branches.

"Steph," Vance shouted from a distance. "Incoming."

Incoming from where?

As she struggled to figure out what he meant, Elizabeth's car appeared above on the steep slope. Ferris had figured out their ruse.

The vehicle was rolling, picking up speed on a direct collision course. He was going to ram them? He'd risk dying in order to punish her? She lunged for Vance's car.

Elizabeth's vehicle careened on, tires crunching. Terror balled her nerves as she ran. There wasn't enough time. She wouldn't be able to open the door and get Chloe to safety before impact.

"Chloe, out," she hollered.

The dog leaped through the window, landed hard on the muddy ground and bolted toward Steph. There was nowhere to go as the oncoming machine plowed into the back of Vance's car, the impact forcing both vehicles onto the bridge. Glass broke with a pop. Momentum fueled the wreck as it was propelled right toward her and Chloe, a massive metal monster. The bridge was too narrow for them to evade the spinning wreck. The opposite end of the bridge was also secured with a sturdy locked gate. Trapped.

Only one answer. Steph leaped onto the metal rail. Below them the water churned, white whorls gleaming. She heard the scream of the tangled vehicles bearing down on them. How deep was the water? How cold? Would she break bones? Be knocked unconscious and drown? Would Chloe be injured in the drop?

No choice.

"Up, Chloe."

The dog did not hesitate to hurl herself into Steph's arms.

Another glance to spot any sign of Vance. But he was nowhere to be seen.

Chloe clutched tight, Steph dropped into the water.

Vance's muscles burned as he ran, hunching over Brutus. He tried to keep to the trees as gunfire rattled from the other side of the trail, the spot where Ferris had positioned Elizabeth's car to careen into his. Likely he'd jammed the gas pedal down somehow. Vance hadn't been able to tell if the crash had caught Steph or Chloe.

He leaped behind a thick trunk as bullets sheared off bits of bark. Brutus trembled. Another round of bullets bored into the trees. Ferris wasn't going to give him the opportunity to take a shot.

He removed Brutus and set him down next to the sling. The dog's brown eyes were pleading. Vance's heart lurched. What had he done dragging a hapless dog into this situation?

"I gotta leave you here, buddy. It's too dangerous for you."

Brutus's whine was pitiful.

He cupped Brutus's hairy muzzle and kissed him on the nose. "I'm real sorry I got you into this, baby. You're a good dog and you should be sitting on a couch next to a fireplace somewhere." He swallowed, moved away and said in his sternest voice, "Stay."

Brutus shivered, but he remained still.

Vance crouched, weapon drawn, and waited. There was no way Ferris would come out in the open and give Vance a shot. He needed a distraction, something to draw Ferris's attention long enough to gain the upper hand.

From the bridge below came the pop of an exploding tire.

Good enough.

Vance put his head down and sprinted

for higher ground, where he could get a bead on Ferris.

A bullet whistled by his ear, so close he could feel the heat trail.

"Next one's in your skull," Ferris called. "Drop the gun."

Running game over. Vance stopped. Slowly he turned, hands up, but he didn't relinquish his weapon. The gun was his only chance to survive long enough to get Steph and the two dogs to safety. He strained to hear any noise from the bridge, praying they'd somehow evaded the crash. The smell of smoke indicated there was a fire burning. That didn't bode well.

Ferris advanced on him, gun held in a neat two-handed grip. "Think your lady's still alive? Or is she a bloody pancake?"

Vance saw a red mist creep over his vision. "You won't win."

"Arrogant, just like I said." Ferris laughed. "Where should I shoot you first? Don't want this to be too easy, do we? More fun when it lasts a while."

"A real party." Vance faced him full on. He was going to take his shot one way or another, though there was zero chance he'd survive. He'd buy time for Steph.

Ferris fired, and Vance grunted as the second bullet whistled by his temple. Ferris laughed.

Something rustled in the bushes.

Ferris darted a quick glance, long enough for Vance to regroup, but as he brought the gun into firing position, Brutus broke from the trees, galloping, the sling caught on his rear leg.

Vance was struck speechless with surprise, unable to shout at the dog to stop. Ferris didn't have time to take proper aim before Brutus bore down on him, barking savagely, saliva dripping. The dog was less than three feet away when the sling finally tangled around his rear paws and he stumbled, somersaulted and crashed right into Ferris's ankles.

They went down in an heap, the gun flying out of Ferris's grip. Brutus scrambled upright again, making a beeline for Vance.

Before Vance could get off a shot, the dog rose up on his hind legs, sling and all, to leap into Vance's arms. *Stop. Sit. Stay.* All the words got fouled in Vance's mouth as the dog hit him like a cannonball. He barely managed to keep on his feet, clutch the animal and maintain his hold on the gun. He finally slapped the drool from his eyes, cinched Brutus under one arm and raised his weapon.

Ferris was gone. His gun too. Vance put Brutus down, then scanned the shrubs. He bit back a shout of frustration. The coward only felt comfortable when he had every advantage. But he hadn't gone far, that was for sure.

Though he longed to charge into the woods after Ferris, he had other priorities. He stuffed the sling into his pocket, called to Brutus, about-faced and sprinted to the bridge.

His pulse was out of control. *Please,*

*Lord, don't let me find them hurt...
or worse.* But when he pulled up at the
wreck, there was no sign that Chloe and
Steph had been caught in the crash. His
smashed car was crookedly wedged between Elizabeth's burning front bum-
per and the bridge supports. The steering
wheel was compacted clear to the dash
and the two front tires were hissing air.
There would be no driving it. Or Elizabeth's car, even if they had the chance.
The hood was billowing smoke.

Their transportation was now gone, but
his thoughts were rushing in one direction
only. He allowed himself five seconds to
reach in through his fractured rear window and grab his pack.

He held his breath against the acrid
smoke as they rushed to the far end of
the bridge, which provided a wider view.
Maybe his movement would broadcast his
position to Ferris, but he didn't see many
options. Steph and Chloe weren't on the

bridge, which meant they'd somehow escaped.

"Steph," he called in a low voice, but louder than the tumbling waves.

The only answer was the roar of the water. Fear flashed like a grenade through him as he scanned. Was the river deep enough for them to have jumped? She'd been wearing heavy boots and clothing. What if…? He freed a flashlight from his pack and swiped it across the dancing surface. The current was ferocious and it might have swept them away, like it had done to Gina. He thought of Gina slipping through his fingers, the strange look in her eyes. Resigned? Angry at her fate?

He was anything but resigned as he shoved down his rising panic. "Steph," he called again, louder. Above the tumult, he heard something. His imagination? But Brutus heard it too. He hauled himself up to brace his front paws on the railing. Vance moved to the dog and craned to look over the side.

"Down here." The voice was barely audible.

The words electrified him, filled him with an eruption of emotion so strong it could have blown off the top of his head. "Where? Where are you?"

"Here," Steph called again.

He almost bent in half over the railing and finally spied her, clinging with trembling arms to one of the cement posts underneath that supported the structure. Chloe was draped across her shoulders and she'd managed to keep hold of her backpack. Brutus shoved his snout around Vance's shin and barked. He felt like barking too.

Steph called up. "Was it Ferris?"

Good question, but not the most important one. Ferris or not, how was he going to get Steph and her dog out? "Coming for you."

With Brutus over his shoulders, he climbed over the barrier and down onto the brushy slope, sliding through mud and debris until they reached the river's edge. He took off his pack. The center support where Steph and Chloe were perched was ten feet from the bank, a stretch of roiling water separating them. He couldn't reach her, even with his long arms, and if he tried to swim, the current might catch him. He was Steph's only chance. And he wasn't convinced that Brutus wouldn't dive right in alongside him. Could the dog swim? He had no idea.

Work smarter, not harder. His gaze raked the underside of the structure.

Bridges required maintenance, tools, equipment. There had to be something he could use. It was almost completely dark, but his flashlight beam provided enough light for him to assess. He spotted a ladder affixed to the underside of the bridge. When the water was lower, it would provide a way for workers to inspect the infrastructure. He slogged through the mud and climbed onto the cement support. A closer inspection revealed the ladder was rusted in places. It flaked under his palms as he grabbed and pulled. The metal groaned but did not come away, so he braced his boot against the cement and heaved again until his joints popped. When he thought his muscles would snap, the ladder broke loose and he stumbled back, clutching a section that had torn free.

Elated, he hauled it to the bank, planted one end down on the ground and levered the other over to Steph. She snagged it and laid it on top of the cement piling. Dangerous, the whole setup. If he crawled over to her, the ladder might not hold under his weight. If she crawled to him with Chloe on her shoulders, they both could tumble in.

And there was the Ferris wild card to consider also.

He turned to Brutus, who was fidgeting uneasily in the mud. The dog hoisted himself up against Vance's thighs, leaving mucky paw prints. "Okay, fella. You were amazing back there with Ferris. If you get a whiff of him, you gotta bark and tell me. Copy that?"

Brutus shot out his tongue and slopped it over Vance's cheek. "All right, well stay out of the way, at least."

"Let's do this," he called to Steph.

Steph lowered herself to hands and knees and eased awkwardly onto the rungs. It lurched under her weight, so he threw himself on his end to hold it steady.

She was breathing hard, her lithe body taut with the effort. Chloe appeared unperturbed, her nostrils sampling the air as the two of them inched along. Did bloodhounds ever give their noses a rest? The metal wobbled and he tensed.

"Almost there," he said through gritted teeth. "Last part's a cakewalk."

She grunted. "Speak for yourself."

Her arms trembled violently now, each lurching movement an extreme effort.

Brutus shook his ears and whined. Was that a Ferris alert? Or Brutus's anxiety spilling out?

Without warning, a rung snapped under Stephs's palm and she flailed. Chloe yipped, sliding. Steph barely grabbed a more secure rung and managed to keep them from plunging into the water. The ladder groaned and twisted, rust flaking off into the darkness. The stressed metal would not stay intact much longer. He felt it begin to snap in half.

He dove, stomach first across the span, desperately holding the failing pieces together. "Climb over me. Quick."

Steph didn't hesitate. She flung herself forward. It required all his strength to maintain his grip. He got her elbow in his ear, a boot in his neck and her knee squarely in his kidneys, but he held on and somehow the ladder stayed in one piece long enough for Steph and Chloe to make it across.

Steph immediately grabbed him by the

belt and helped him scramble off. The metal gave way the moment he touched land, breaking into pieces, and was sucked into the maw of the river.

They both doubled over, heaving in oxygen, while Brutus shoved his nose into Chloe's face and began to lick her muzzle. Vance couldn't allow them much recuperation time. Instead, he hustled them under the cover of the thickest tree with the most branches that he could find. He listened hard, but with the water and his own labored breathing, he heard no sign of their stalker.

"What?" she panted. "Ferris?"

He provided the main points of his previous encounter as he stripped off his jacket and wrapped it around her.

Steph's eyes were enormous as she listened to his whispered report. "You're saying..." She looked at Brutus. "That dog took on Ferris?"

Of all the things he'd said, *that* was the one that shocked her? "Yes." There was no need to bring up the fact that the dog had been tangled in the sling and almost wiped Vance out in his exuberance along with Ferris. "But the main point here is Ferris hasn't gone far and we need to move. Are you hurt?"

She shook her head, but she was still staring at Brutus in utter bewilderment as she removed a towel from her waterproof pack to scrub Chloe dry. "He actually attacked Ferris?"

"Plans, Wolfe," he snapped. "We need plans. Focus, would you?"

She heaved out a breath. "What do we have for weaponry?"

"My handgun and yours. Extra clips. Dunno what else you brought."

"Just my Glock. Hopefully still operational." She stowed the damp towel. "Options are to skirt the canyon and bypass the bridge. Get to the main road."

"Sketchy," Vance said. "He's the kind of guy who travels prepared. It's possible he's got another vehicle stashed and he's got the spark plugs for yours. We're both wet and we've got—"

"Two backpacks, a tracking dog and…" She waved a palm at Brutus. "Another dog."

He arched an eyebrow. "New idea. We go for Gina's Jeep."

Steph was quiet for a moment. "If we could make it, it'd get us some wheels. But maybe your car or Elizabeth's is drivable. At least we should check for a working radio."

He shook his head. "They're both burning and it's not worth the risk. Ferris hasn't gone far."

Her chin went up. "It is worth the risk. I can sneak up there while you watch the dogs. Neither one is alerting right now. Ferris probably went to higher ground to spot us."

"Probably?" He fisted his hands on his hips. "I disagree but if you're going to be all stubborn about this, I'll go."

Brutus shook himself and yowled.

Chloe stiffened, nose to the air.

Vance's gut knotted and he went for his gun. Neither plan was going to make a difference if Ferris was in a good firing position.

Ferris's shout drifted down from above. "I'm going to kill both of you."

Vance couldn't see him, but he guessed Ferris was perched on a rocky outcropping twenty yards above their location. Fortunately, he wouldn't be able to spot them from his vantage point thanks to the canopy. Hopefully.

Brutus started to let out a bark, but Vance clapped a hand over his muzzle.

"I'll let you linger on a while, like my father did in prison," Ferris called. "He died. You'll die. No help, no other search and rescue teams around, no Elizabeth. How's that feel?"

Steph locked eyes with Vance. He knew she was calculating the distance, possible escape routes, formulating and rejecting plans like he was.

"I'm going to enjoy every minute of your suffering." Ferris laughed. "Not so cocky without your radios and equipment and your squad, are you? Just two mice with a cat on your tail—a big, nasty, feral cat."

She held up a finger and pointed behind herself, to a gap in the brush that would take them away from the bridge. He nodded, shouldered his pack and settled Brutus under his arm. Their situation was coming into dire focus.

They truly were alone in the Lost Sierra with no vehicle, no communication, only the supplies in their packs, two dogs and a cold-blooded killer on their trail.

Outgunned.

Minimal chance of survival.

Maximum exposure and risk.

He heard Lettie's words, the ones she'd whispered over him as he hunched on his knees, sobbing. *Keep your eyes on the Lord, not on the difficulties.*

Steph was looking at him. He squared his shoulders and answered her slight nod with one of his own. *Lord, here we go.*

He followed her into the trees, Ferris's laughter ringing in his ears.

FIVE

They didn't speak. It took all their faculties to move through the thick trees, skirting rocks and avoiding the thorn-studded clumps of shrubbery. Steph's half-frozen brain struggled to take it all in. One moment she was looking forward to a competition challenge and the next she was fighting for survival. And not by herself either.

Vance plowed along with apparent ease, which made her pick up the pace a tic in spite of the numbness of her limbs. She wasn't about to lag behind.

God must have a rich sense of humor to put her into this situation with Vance. Anyone else would have been more welcome than the big man striding along in front of her, muttering reassurances to his nervous wreck of a dog. Was she supposed to learn some lesson about being forced to cooperate with the guy she'd sooner leave in the dust? She slapped at a branch. There would be no learning, only tolerating. Temporary allies, that was all. Or more like cooperative enemies.

Their silent hike lasted two hours, with only occasional stops for reconnoitering and sips of water. Sprinkles turned into drizzle, freezing drops chilling whatever parts the dive into the river hadn't. She had hand and feet warmers in her pack, but there was no sense activating those until they stopped. Her toes had gone numb the moment she'd jumped off the bridge into the water.

Chloe was undaunted. Keeping her canine companion cool during sweltering days was more of a concern than the opposite, but the dog was no doubt tiring, since Steph wasn't hauling her up the steep stretches like Vance was doing for

Brutus. They were easing along a rugged uphill section when Chloe lost her footing and began to slide. Steph caught her harness and pulled her close.

"Gotcha, Chloe." The dog licked her face. Steph used the break to take a quick peek at the map, cupping the light with her palm and checking her compass.

"Jeep's another two miles," she said, heart sinking. "Uphill."

He swatted a bug from his brow. Now that he was facing her, she was gratified to read fatigue on his features too. Her body was screaming for rest and warmth, relief of any kind.

"We gotta stop," he said. "Find a place to hunker for the night. Hope Ferris has done the same."

Thoughts of Ferris's chilling promise made her want to keep moving, but Vance was right. It was almost certain that she or Vance or one of the dogs would get hurt trying to navigate. And the drizzle had morphed into a downpour. She could no longer control her shivering. Since Vance had given her his jacket, his sweatshirt was soaked. He had to be freezing as well. Brutus was no petite canine and lugging the dog was a workout. Rest was imperative. *No alternative, Stephanie.* Jaw clamped, she nodded in agreement.

Vance pulled a flashlight from his back pocket and she was going to caution him when he shielded it with his hand as he beamed it around. Unlikely as it was that Ferris could detect the meager gleam through all the foliage, they couldn't take the risk. He explored the shrubs and rocks beyond while she shifted from foot to foot to try to restore circulation.

An eternity later, he reappeared. "Found a place. Come on."

Knees shaking, she followed him through the sheeting rain.

He pushed aside the wet foliage and led them toward a cliff of rock. At first, she could see nothing through the increasing rain, but he guided them to a cleft of granite, a dark pocket shielded from the elements by a jutting slab above. He bent almost in half and disappeared inside. She followed with Chloe.

The interior was cold, the rock ceiling no more than six feet high, but the ten-foot patch of earth that served as a floor was dry and she was deliriously delighted to be out of the rain. Chloe flapped the water from her ears and sank down next to Brutus. Both dogs were tired to the point of exhaustion, much like their humans.

She tried to channel the water funneling from her borrowed jacket into an out-of-the-way spot.

"You have a change of clothes?" Vance hunched to keep from banging his head.

"Of course. You?"

"Yep. You first." He turned his back and she slunk into the darkest corner of the cave, rifled through her pack and swapped her wet clothes for the dry ones. It was pure bliss to yank on the socks and her backup boots, even though she could hardly feel her feet. She returned the jacket to Vance. He changed his own clothes, exclaiming as he banged his elbows and head in the cramped space. They both rubbed down the dogs with dry towels. Chloe submitted gracefully. Brutus rolled onto his back, legs splayed, and begged for additional tummy rubs, which Vance supplied.

"You're Daddy's good boy," he crooned. "Tough as nails, right?"

Her watch read almost 10:00 p.m. Seemed like they'd been hiking a lot longer than that. She began to unpack some of her supplies, jittery at having Vance so close. Normally on a mission, it would be only her and Chloe. All of her siblings, with the exception of Kara, preferred working alone. Different case now. While she knew she would be twice as vulnerable without Vance, her nerves refused to settle. He seemed to take up so much of the space in the cave, his presence impossible to ignore. She caught the scent of the woods that clung to him, the droplets that hung from his shorn blond hair. Was that an empty snack-food wrapper that had fallen from his pocket when he changed?

A memory lit her consciousness like a streetlamp turning on at dusk.

Cookies.

One of their fellow officer's kids, Jaycie, had been trying to sell cookies for her Girl Scout troop, but there was stiff competition in her neighborhood from a group of girls who'd bullied Jaycie at school. Vance had immediately purchased all seventy boxes of cookies on the spot, spending his entire monthly food budget. After that, she'd known whenever she was invited over for dinner they would be eating boxed mac and cheese with Scout cookies for dessert. The memory left a complex aftertaste, both bitter and sweet.

Why was she thinking about that now? Her business was survival. No bandwidth for anything else. "I'm disoriented, but at first light I'll climb and get us a bearing."

He didn't argue, kneeling and rifling

through his pack. He pulled a packet free, unfurled a packable bowl and dumped in kibble for Brutus. It pleased her that he'd prioritized the needs of his dog. She suspected he'd taken on Brutus to help his cover when he entered the tracking competition. So was Brutus merely a means to an end, or a companion? She'd get the truth about him one way or another.

Brutus gazed at Vance as he filled an additional water bowl while she did the same for Chloe.

"Go ahead, Brutus," Vance said. "Eat up."

The dog cocked his head, unmoving.

Vance shifted and spoke louder. "Brutus, chow time."

Chloe munched her food and they both eyed Vance and his dog.

Brutus didn't seem inclined to move. "He's your cover, isn't he? You got him recently? He's not a tracking dog, obviously."

"Well, no. Not exactly a tracker. I got

him at the shelter. Figured if I showed up at the competition without a dog, they'd get suspicious."

Bingo. Typical Vance, making an impulsive decision. Did he realize that Brutus was now his lifetime responsibility? He'd better. No way would she hear of him dumping the dog if they managed to survive.

Brutus was still staring at Vance. "Maybe he does have some training," Steph said. "He looks like he's waiting for you to give him permission to eat."

"We're still getting to know each other. It's only been a couple of weeks. Permission granted, Brutus," Vance said. "Eat, huh?"

Instead, the dog laid his fleshy head on his paws and stared forlornly at Vance, who rubbed a palm over the back of his neck. "I, uh, actually, I think maybe I've confused him."

Whatever the issue was, Vance was not keen on telling her. Silently, she waited.

He looked everywhere but at Stephanie. "The thing is, his name's not actually Brutus, according to the shelter."

"What is it?"

"I, um, I'm not sure I can recall."

She folded her arms and skewered him with a look. "Don't lie."

He searched for a spot on the ceiling and exhaled. "It's Pudge."

The dog looked brightly at Vance, tail wagging. Vance sighed. "Sorry, boy. Wrong of me to change that on you, wasn't it? Eat, Pudge."

The dog practically dove into his food bowl. Kibble flew as he wolfed it down noisily.

Stephanie giggled. "Now that name suits him."

Vance rolled his eyes. "Yeah, well, what self-respecting champion tracker is named Pudge? I had to think of something else."

Her giggles turned into guffaws and escalated from there until tears streamed down her cheeks. Probably a release from the tension they'd just experienced, but she couldn't stop for several minutes.

Vance laughed too. "Pudge has had a tough transition. He lived on a fishing boat and it was a quiet life, you know? But his owner passed away and he landed in the shelter and no one wanted him for some reason. And there was this big, alpha dog in the cage next to him, and Pudge is, you know, sensitive. I could see he had potential, though."

"He's..." She was going to remark that Pudge had a snowball's chance in the desert of turning into a tracking dog, but instead she cleared her throat. "He's got some good instincts."

Vance beamed, looking like a schoolboy who had won the spelling bee. "Really? You think so?" An errant bit of kibble dropped from Pudge's fleshy lips and he gobbled it up before wagging his tail at Vance. He massaged Pudge's neck until the dog's rear leg pistoned in pleasure. "I thought he looked intelligent. Mostly desperate, but with undertones of intelligence."

Steph watched the tender smile play across Vance's lips. He obviously did care about this animal. A strange feeling of fondness crept over her for this big, muscled man with a heart of butter. What? Hard stop right there. No matter how much of a dog lover he turned out to be, he was also a manipulator who'd betrayed her and decided to track Ferris on his own without seeing fit to let her know. Even if she had blocked his calls, he could have gotten her the message.

Didn't think she could take care of business herself?

A misperception she'd fought her whole career. Women had to walk a tightrope in the workplace that men would never encounter. Come across too tough and you were seen as abrasive. Too emotional and you were a liability. He wouldn't ever understand because police work was still a largely male profession. That's why it was even more painful to be cheated out of a rare chance at promotion.

What was all this useless cogitating while they were being hunted like animals? She brought out her topo map and spread it on the ground, examining it with her penlight. Her cheeks were tight with cold. It would be amazing to light a fire, but she didn't feel confident they'd put enough distance between them and Ferris. She still wondered about the guy on horseback too—Evan from the registration area. Something about him bothered her. His rude comment felt out of place with the enthusiastic, positive people who usually participated in search and rescue events.

Vance began rattling things around, but she was determined to focus and ignore him as much as possible. She located the ambush spot where Gina's Jeep was parked. But where were she and Vance, exactly? She could hazard a guess, but she wouldn't be certain until daybreak, when the rising sun would be an advantage and a hindrance. If she could get a view of the area, so could Ferris. But all she needed was some intel and a few seconds of signal to text her family. Once they alerted Security Hounds, she and Vance could evade Ferris until help arrived. Her mother, Beth, and siblings Kara, Garrett, Chase and Roman, and their assorted dogs would move mountains to get to them.

A sizzle of lightning lit the cave. Seconds later thunder rolled overhead and Pudge yelped. Since Vance was still busy with something or other, Pudge scooted next to Chloe who laid her head over his neck. Both dogs closed their eyes. If that wasn't adorable.

Don't get attached to Vance's dog, Chloe. This isn't a permanent thing. Pudge certainly had no such reservations. He practically had cartoon hearts in his eyes when he gazed at Chloe. She covered both animals with a lightweight blanket from her pack.

Finally, she looked up to find Vance tinkering with a portable butane stove. She watched as he poured water into a metal bowl and turned up the flame. As if her limbs had a mind of their own, she found herself moving toward that comforting glow.

"What are you doing?" she said.

"Making dinner for the humans."

Dinner? Food felt like a trivial matter in light of their situation, but her stomach was growling like a bear coming out of hibernation. Wouldn't do them any good to starve. She had more than enough for the competition, but it didn't hurt to be cautious with their supplies. No doubt Ferris had packed enough food to see him through his deadly mission. Besides, if Vance was willing to cook, she was happy to gobble down whatever he provided.

He might as well have been a scientist fusing atoms, so closely did he watch the bubbling water. After a few minutes he turned off the flame and poured the hot liquid into metal cups, then ripped open two packets of instant oatmeal and dumped them in. He sank a metal spoon into both and handed one over.

"Oh, wait. One sec." From another bag, he sprinkled M&M's into the oatmeal. "For flavor," he said.

Her eyes flew wide. Vance was an unrepentant sugar addict. She'd schooled him on the subject repeatedly, along with other warnings, but as the warm oatmeal melted the chocolate into colorful swirls, she could think of nothing else she'd rather eat.

They sat cross-legged with her small solar lantern partially covered between them.

"Thank you, Father, that we're alive, the dogs are alive and You've provided this food." He added a plea for their safety and for the families of Elizabeth and Gina, which made her eyes pool. Ferris had killed two women, if Gina had succumbed to the river. And he was ready to kill two more people if they gave him the chance.

"You should have told me you were after him."

He sighed. "We already skied that slope."

She hesitated. "My brother warned me not to enter this contest. Now I wish I'd listened, but Ferris would have found me anyway." She shrugged. "I got some anonymous threats. No doubt it was him."

"Did you go to the cops?"

"No." She countered, "Did you ever fill them in on your investigations? Did they know you made it your personal mission to get the dirt on him?"

He looked down. "No."

"Why not?"

He dragged his gaze to hers. "I didn't get Ferris when I should have. That's on me. I…" He swallowed. "I did a lot of things I regret, Steph. None more than how I treated you."

Warmth crept up her neck. "We don't need to go into that."

"I'd like to. I have some damage to repair," he said softly.

"What makes you think it's repairable?"

The silence magnified until it filled the whole space.

She shrugged. "Let's just eat, okay? Before it gets cold."

They dug into the oatmeal. The creamy mass was sweet and comforting. It was all she could do to keep from moaning aloud as she savored. She ate every morsel, the warm goo restoring her an inch at a time.

Vance sighed as he scraped up the last remnant. "Wish I could have seconds, but that should take the edge off."

"Thank you, for…you know, cooking dinner."

He smiled, showing the dimple in spite of his five-o'clock shadow. "You're welcome. Glad I bought some of those premade camping-meal packs. The candy was my brilliant addition, of course, and not to toot my own horn but that really made the meal."

She wouldn't say so, but he was right. Her supplies were nourishing, top notch nutritionally, but the chocolate was still dancing on her tongue.

He reached for her and her mouth went dry. What was he…?

He eased a twig from her hair. "Brought some of the forest with you."

She ducked her chin, mortified, because in that moment she realized she'd wanted him to touch her, to trace a finger along her cheek like he'd done when they dated. She gulped and found a wipe in her bag to clean out the cups. He tried to stop her.

"Only fair I do the dishes," she insisted, "since you cooked."

He yawned and tried to stretch, but there wasn't room. "I'll keep watch. You get some shut-eye."

"I…" Rest was imperative. They had a long hike to the Jeep. Exhaustion was already dulling her senses. "Okay." She set her watch alarm. "An hour. Then we switch."

"Two."

"Do you have to argue about everything?"

"Two," he insisted, "or you'll be cranky."

And in that maddening way of his, he moved on, smoothed out a spot in the dirt for himself to sit and zipped his spare jacket. He crammed on a black ski cap.

"'Night, Steph."

"Good night."

While she wiped out the cups, his comment twirled through her mind.

I have some damage to repair.

He acknowledged he'd done wrong. She suspected that was the reason he'd called her endless times, leaving messages on her cell that she'd not returned. *Fool me once*, she'd told herself. What would he have said if she'd allowed him to speak? she wondered. And how would she have felt about it?

The chill from the stone permeated her

clothes and left her squeezing the emergency blanket tighter around herself. She didn't think she would be able to sleep with the cold and Ferris and the hard floor. But for some reason, as she stared at Vance's silhouetted profile, her body eased itself into oblivion.

SIX

Vance dimly remembered taking over the watch from Steph in the wee hours. He must have dozed momentarily, yanking himself awake to find Pudge curled up beside him, Chloe and Steph gone.

His heart lurched until he realized it was nearly 4:00 a.m. and she'd likely gone outside to pinpoint their exact location, like she'd told him she would. He forced himself fully awake. Every muscle and joint hollered at him and it was an effort to heave himself upright. And he barely avoided slamming his skull on the low ceiling. They went outside, where he found a place for morning business. Pudge meandered through some wet foliage to stretch his legs, but he didn't go far. The temperature was enough to make his teeth chatter, the heavy atmosphere oppressive. The rain was sparse, but the air was thick with the promise of more. Watery pockets of moonlight peeked from behind undulating clouds. The gist of it was they were going to get pounded today. No getting around that.

"Hope you don't mind being wet, fella."

Pudge flapped his ears. One stood up and the other was at half-mast. Nothing about that dog was perfectly symmetrical. Chloe hadn't seemed to care. "I think you might have a shot with Chloe, you know, if you mind your p's and q's." The canine relationship was moving more smoothly than his and Steph's, but he was fairly certain they'd crossed a barrier the day before. At least she was speaking to him. And he no longer had to try and keep up his dog's alias.

He tried his phone. No bars.

Steph and Chloe appeared. Pudge scurried up to sniff his dog partner.

Vance raised a hand in greeting. "Success?"

"Yes and no. Got our location. Still not able to call or message. It's about a mile and a half to the Jeep. Steep."

He tried to hold in his groan. That was an hour hike in the best of conditions. "How exposed is the route between here and there?"

"Concealed until we reach the lip of the valley where we have to drop down into the meadow. That's going to put us in plain view for a solid quarter mile unless..."

"Unless?"

"We can take another route that loops around to the eastern side and access the meadow that way, but it's rugged and longer. It will add on an hour minimum, probably two."

Another couple of hours for them to be discovered and killed. Would they be better off extending the time until they could secure transportation or get there faster with greater risk of being spotted? A coin flip, at best. "All right. We can delay that decision until we reach the edge of the valley though, right?"

"Agreed."

His stomach growled. "More important question before we break camp. Breakfast or no breakfast? I've got M&M's and two more packets of oatmeal left if we can spare ten minutes."

A flicker of moonlight drifting between the clouds softened her expression, or maybe it was his imagination.

She chuckled. "Always the chow hound."

He grinned and stretched his bruised muscles. "I learned a long time ago, if I'm going on a hike with you, best to fuel up first."

Her smile remained for a moment and he held his breath. He'd lived for that smile in the past, ached for it after she'd left the force, left him. Her mind might have been drifting through the memories too because her smile drained away, tucked behind a serious get-it-done look that shut the door on their intimacy. *Just as well. Wasn't it? Bigger fish to fry, Vance? Stuff like survival?*

"We shouldn't take the time for us to eat. Just feed the dogs. We can have a snack later," she pronounced.

His protesting stomach disagreed but he offered a thumbs-up. They packed quickly, fed and watered the dogs, checked their weapons and departed. He was happy to let her lead. He could read a topo map just fine, but she had way more experience in the wilderness than he did. Steph was smart and strong. And funny, at the most unexpected moments, like the time she'd whipped three clementines off the staff-room table and showed off the juggling skills her brother Chase had taught her. The performance earned her the nickname of Steph the Magnificent. A random moment that he couldn't stop reliving.

He zipped his jacket and fell in behind her.

Pudge seemed content to walk today, as

long as he was within touching distance of Chloe. Vance appreciated the break for his biceps, which still ached from lugging the dog the day before.

The route was uneven, puddled with rainwater that threatened to soak them to their ankles if they didn't pay attention. The dogs had the uncanny knack of avoiding the squishier areas and he only had to help Pudge off an unsteady rock once while Chloe waited patiently, wagging her tail in encouragement. Maybe Pudge was going to turn into a more confident canine after all, under her tutelage. They kept on until the rain started again and they pulled up under some dripping trees for a rest. Pudge immediately scooted with Chloe under a thick mat of branches.

Steph looked as winded as he felt. Water funneled down her hood, dampening the fringe of dark bangs as they joined the dogs under the shelter.

"Breakfast break?" he asked.

"Something quick."

While he fished through his pack, she pulled out a lined, water-repellent vest and fastened it around Chloe. "Didn't you bring rain gear for Pudge?"

He frowned. "No. I didn't think of it."

She blew out an exasperated breath. "When you have a dog, you have to plan ahead, Vance. It's like bringing a child along."

"I did plan, kinda, but it didn't occur to me we'd be stuck in a downpour."

"Planning for the future isn't your forte," she muttered.

He felt a lash of irritation. "I was busy thinking about killers and such, you know?"

She wiped the water from her hood. "That excuse won't hold up. It's your modus operandi, Vance, and you know it."

"What is?" He was uncomfortable now, cold and hungry. Not the best time for the argument she'd started.

"A lack of preparation." She shoved her wet hood back from her brow.

He stared. "Just because I don't overthink every life decision like you do, doesn't make me—"

"You lease cars and get rid of them. You never wanted to talk about settling down in a place. You spend every dollar you earn."

Not the first time he'd heard her say that. It had been a bone of contention between them during the six months they'd dated. He looked at the strange assortment of things he'd shoved into the backpack and at his dripping dog. Arguing, especially about this topic, was not helpful. He tried to turn it into a joke. "Spontaneous. That's what makes me the life of the party."

No return smile. She wasn't going to be diverted and she shook her head, which annoyed him further. So he wasn't a seasoned wilderness searcher. He'd brought candy for the oatmeal and kibble and water, hadn't he? The most important stuff. He took a deep breath and let it out. "Okay. So the future is the last thing on my mind sometimes. Is that a crime?"

She faced him, fists on hips. They stared at each other, ire simmering between them until she surprised him by heaving out a defeated breath. Her expression wasn't as much angry as desiring an answer. To what question, he wasn't sure.

"Why, Vance? The reluctance to entertain the future and long-range plans and all that. Why was it always the last thing on your mind?" Moisture spangled her lashes and a raindrop landed on her cheek. Without thinking, he reached and thumbed it away, her skin like chilled satin to his touch.

She didn't move, just stood still, waiting.

He was uncertain how to reply. "Because I didn't... I don't..."

She continued her silent stare. He was not going to get out of answering. Might as well come clean. Could be the only chance he ever got to do so. "I used to have everything planned out when I was in the Marines. I saved up my pay and invested it, believe it or not. Stocks, bonds, 401(k), the whole nine."

Clearly, she didn't believe it from the sudden dropping open of her mouth.

"My plan was to take care of my mom. She was my hero. My dad took off when I was three and she managed everything herself my whole life. We were really close." He fought down the lump in his throat. "I knew when I enlisted it would be hard on her, having me away, but I had this plan, see? I'd come out with a nest egg, use the GI Bill to pay for school and buy Mom a nicer place, with the garden she always wanted. I'd take care of all the maintenance and yard work and everything." He almost threw the words at her. "See that? Buttoned-up, adult-type plans, right?"

She cocked her head. "But it didn't happen."

He stared, unfocused, at the lashing rain. "No." The weight of his mother's situation crashed down on his soul again, pressing the anger away in a well of defeat. "I came home and two months later she was diagnosed with Alzheimer's. Four months after that and she didn't know me. I could have handled it I think, except that it changed her whole personality. She acted as if she hated me." He swallowed the bile. "She… called me a loser, accused me of trying to steal her money. Threw shoes at me. Who knew she had a killer throwing arm?" Not funny, but he'd tried.

Steph recoiled. "That's awful, Vance."

"Yes. Nothing to be done about it. It wasn't her, it was the disease, but…" He took a breath. "I promised her since I was five years old that I'd take care of her and never put her in a home. I tried so hard." He kept his voice steady in spite of the pain. *So. Hard.*

She touched his hand and he stared at their connection, the small, strong fingers.

"Sounds like you didn't have a choice." Her tone was so soft it made him ache inside.

He shook his head. "I managed for a year, with Aunt Lettie's help. You remember me talking about Lettie?"

Steph nodded. The older lady, not actually a blood relation, had become somewhat of a mother figure to Vance, she knew that much.

"Lettie came over every day after her son, Jack, left for work. She cooked and helped me cajole Mom into going to her doctor appointments, sat with us while we watched the same recorded game show over and over. Showed me how to sneak Mom's medicines into foods she liked. She'd play the piano, which soothed Mom usually. When it got too dangerous and Mom went to the facility, Lettie still came over, every single day." His cheeks burned. "I was drinking a lot then, and she'd come and pray over me and make sure I ate. After Mom passed, she even drove me to meetings until I could stay sober on my own."

He didn't want to meet Steph's eyes,

fearing what he might see. "After that…" He lifted a shoulder. "I don't know. It seemed like my plans all went up in smoke. I couldn't keep my promise to my mother. I lost my taste for thinking about a future. Lettie said someday God would give me a reason to look ahead again." Now he dared a glance and did not find pity or scorn in her expression, which heartened him. "And then when I couldn't keep my promise to Lettie about putting Ferris away…"

Her brow furrowed as she put the pieces together. "It was her son who tipped the Grinders off that their employee Harlow was going to talk to the cops."

He scrubbed a hand over his face. "Yes, it was. Jack was her only child. Ferris pressured him into spying on the Grinders' employees if he wanted to keep his job. Jack felt he had no choice but to report that Lawrence Harlow was going to contact the police. Then they wound up killed. After the family was murdered, Jack couldn't take the guilt. Lettie found him after he overdosed on sleeping pills."

Steph exhaled. "Tragic. Lettie must have been devastated."

"After everything she did for me, I couldn't ease her pain in any way but one." Now he held his breath as he watched her.

"You promised to make sure Ferris went to prison for what he'd done," she said finally.

"I was desperate to make it happen. I got the detective's job, but all I could hang on Ferris was fraud. No solid proof that he was responsible for the executions. No physical evidence to put him at the scene."

"Lettie doesn't blame you for not getting Ferris for murder, does she?"

"No. She doesn't have to." Because he blamed himself.

The moment had come. God had made it happen in this bizarre set of circumstances. He'd have his chance to say what he'd been composing in his heart for a year and a half. "For what it's worth, Steph, and I know that's not much, I am sincerely sorry for taking the job that you should have had. More than that, way more, it was wrong of me to share your personal information to better my chances, telling the chief you were interviewing elsewhere. I still can't believe I actually did that. I'm ashamed. It was wrong. I'm sorry."

Her lips went tight and she looked down at the sodden ground. The silence stretched long between them. He'd apologized. She hadn't accepted. When he realized she wasn't going to reply, he started up again.

"Hey, what am I going on about? You asked why I'm no good at adulting and I'm blabbing my life story." "Blabbing" was the right word. He couldn't stop the nervous gush of speech now. "I'm working on being a better grown-up. Probably won't impress you that I opened a savings account and drew up plans to build a house on a piece of property my uncle deeded me in Whisper Valley."

She jerked a look at him. "Really?"

"Yeah. Going to build a mother-in-law unit too, if I can convince Aunt Lettie to come live in it." He forced a smile. "Doing some adulting, right? Better late than never."

"Yes."

She fiddled with the zipper on her backpack. He resolved to keep to the important details and stuff the personal comments down deep.

She finally spoke without actually looking at him. "But just doubling back, your plans collapsed, but the important thing is your mother knew you loved her."

Surprised, he gaped at her. "How do you know?"

"Know what?"

"That my mom, even with the way she was, knew I loved her? Because I was so frustrated, angry when she'd go at me.

How would she know?" He yearned for her answer.

"She saw what you did, the actions."

"But she sure didn't appreciate some of them."

"Maybe not, but deep down she knew. We think love is a feeling, but that's not the whole truth. Love is action, behavior—it's what you do when you aren't feeling the good feelings."

He cocked his head at her, wanting more.

"You cared for her when she threw shoes at you."

"Yes."

"You showed her she was special, cooked for her, read to her, turned on her favorite game shows even though they were repeats and you'd probably seen them a million times."

"Uh-huh."

"That's God's kind of love, Vance. Honoring and respecting in spite of your feelings, not because of them."

He wanted to touch her shoulder, turn her to face him. Instead, he stood beside her, lost in wonder. "Who taught you that?"

"Mom's a big one for the Bible stuff. Let's redistribute the wealth here." She bent and removed Chloe's rain vest, stripped off the underneath liner and put the outer layer back on her. Then she stopped to fasten the inner part around Pudge. It barely held around his stocky tummy. "There. We'll improvise so they'll both stay somewhat dry."

"Thank you." He grinned at his ungainly dog. "You like it, Pudgy?"

Pudge flapped his ears and wriggled his tush.

Steph gave each dog a jerky treat, which they accepted with tail wags. She fidgeted with her bag of goodies. "I'm sorry I badgered you about the planning thing," she said finally. "I can be bossy to the point of meanness. Something I need to work on. And…" She gazed at him with those smoky eyes and his heart lurched. "I'm truly sorry about your mother, Vance. You did everything you could and she knew that deep down."

And then she hugged him. He had to be dreaming, but there she was, her arms encircling him. His head dropped and he laid his cheek on her shoulder. She held him close. He took it in, the comfort of her presence, a flood of connection that made him want to sob and laugh at the same moment. All too soon, she let him go, busying herself stowing her materials.

He steadied himself with a deep breath. Though she hadn't actually accepted his apology verbally, somehow he felt they'd reached a precarious place of understanding. Strange that they'd attain it here, in the middle of a manhunt, one step ahead of an assassin.

To hide his discomfiture, he snagged two items from his backpack. "Peanut-butter crackers. Acceptable breakfast?"

"I've got some protein bars…"

"No offense, but these are going to taste better."

He held one out to her, but a sound made him tense.

She looked around. "What?"

He put a finger to his lips and whispered. "Thought I heard something."

They stood motionless for several minutes. Wind spit rain under the branches at them. Chloe cocked an ear, alert but not overly so. "False alarm, I guess."

He offered the crackers again. "Would be better with grape jelly."

"It'll do." She took the crackers, touched his biceps with her free hand and squeezed, her fingers tracing warmth throughout his body. Another physical gesture? He must be on a roll. Or she was getting loopy from hunger and exertion.

"I love peanut-butter crackers," she told him. "Maybe there's something to be said for letting the seat-of-the-pants guy plan the meals."

"Score one for the Marines."

"Don't get your ego puffed up about it."

"Too late."

He wished they could stay like this, enjoying an easiness between them he'd never dared imagine he'd experience again. She unwrapped the cellophane and popped a cracker into her mouth. The ground was wet, so they leaned with their backs against a smooth tree trunk, which kept them mostly sheltered from the elements.

He was devouring his second cracker when Chloe leaped to her feet, nose in the air. Pudge followed suit a moment later. On high alert, all four of them stared into the rain. The noise became more defined, the same low buzzing he thought he'd heard earlier.

Now he could not ignore the facts.

The buzzing was not from anything in the natural environment.

Fifteen feet away, the black metal drone appeared and disappeared, skirting the edge of the forest like a man-made dragonfly.

His stomach dropped.

They were about to be discovered.

Steph silenced Chloe with a signal and put a palm on Pudge to keep him quiet. She and Vance slowly drew the dogs back farther into the bushes, the wet branches clawing and scratching. In her haste to snatch up their belongings, she prayed she'd not left anything that might be visible to the spy.

Ferris had a drone. Why should she be surprised? The lightweight flying machines equipped with cameras were still a fairly new phenomenon when she'd left the force, so she only knew the rudimentary facts, but they'd grown to be outrageously common. Her brother Chase had a toy model that he sometimes took on training runs to track their bloodhound's progress. Drones were equipped with high-tech cameras that streamed real-time videos and could be purchased on the cheap. They could be flown anywhere by a skilled operator, as long as the batteries remained charged. Some had fancy thermal imaging to detect body heat. If this drone had that capability, their goose was cooked.

"It's a low-grade model," Vance whispered in her ear, tickling her cheek. "Probably has a four-hundred-meter range."

The number made her gut quiver. That meant the drone operator, the man who wanted them dead, was less than a half mile away. A thought occurred to her. "Is it possible he has an accomplice?"

Vance frowned. "I didn't want to bring that up, but it occurred to me too."

"Could be Ferris himself flying it, or the guy I encountered on the way in. Evan. He was on horseback. Something about him rubbed me the wrong way. What was it?" She closed her eyes trying to recall him in detail. "I got it. His name tag was pristine, the lanyard too. Elizabeth's was banged up. Obviously she was with the group a long time."

"Not conclusive, but food for thought."

She peered at the drone. "Do you think it spotted us?"

"We'll find out pretty soon."

They crouched in the scratchy, dripping shrubbery and waited. She had her arms around the dogs and they were intensely focused on the whining intruder, but quiet, as she'd directed them to be.

"Good dogs." She stroked their heads. "It'll be okay."

But would it? If Ferris knew exactly where they were?

The drone whizzed along, approaching the trees but not moving too close to the canopy.

"He can't risk clipping a branch so he's got to keep clear," Vance said.

She realized she was holding her breath and forced herself to exhale. Her watch ticked off the minutes as the drone hummed around them. Five, eight, ten, twelve. Her calves cramped and a drop of freezing water slithered down the neck of her jacket.

The whining motor hitched into a slightly different octave.

"Battery's low," Vance murmured. "Cheap ones can only last about forty minutes before they have to be recharged or switched out for a new one."

Vance was a whiz on this drone stuff.

The drone completed one more erratic search and then retreated, vanishing behind the distant hillside. With one finger, Vance gave her the wait signal. They remained immobile until he unfolded himself and crept free from the bushes. She followed suit with the dogs, but they remained beneath the shelter of the trees.

Vance peered at the sky. "Don't think he spotted us."

"But we can't risk taking the exposed path to the Jeep. Not with a drone in the picture."

Distracted, he pulled a broken peanut-butter cracker from his jacket pocket and ate it in one bite. "Looks like it's the long way around for us, huh?"

She heaved a sigh. "'Fraid so. We'd best get moving before he has his drone operating again."

They cautiously eased back onto the path and soon tackled the sharp slope that would lead them in a circuitous route to the meadow.

"It'll all be worth it if we can get ourselves a set of wheels," Vance said.

With a vehicle, they'd stand a chance.

But if Ferris could track them with the drone, would he suspect they were headed for Gina's abandoned Jeep?

If so, they were on their way to another ambush.

And the chances they'd survive diminished with every passing moment.

SEVEN

Vance and Steph stopped regularly to rest, water and feed the dogs and refresh themselves. Twice they dove into the bushes when they thought they'd heard the approach of the drone, but both occasions had turned out to be nothing but delays.

His calves were screaming at him, along with various other body parts. Hopefully, he'd done a fair job concealing his aches and pains throughout their arduous march. Going uphill was a tremendous effort and he'd had to carry Pudge, who'd become exhausted in spite of his stiff-upper-lip attitude. At least Vance's thoughts were a good distraction from the physical misery.

The hiking provided plenty of time to consider what had transpired between him and Steph since he'd shown up at the competition starting line. He still wasn't sure exactly how to categorize their conversations. Healing? Confrontational? Cathartic? He'd never wanted to tell her about his mother, but she'd reacted with surprising understanding and tenderness, and he felt lighter for it. She'd accepted his apology, and though she'd clearly not forgiven him, she'd at least listened. As he reached to help her and Chloe over a sharp spine of rock, he imagined what it would feel like to hold her hand on a regular basis. She braced against his arm as she climbed over the obstacle. His fancy, no doubt, but he thought she might have allowed her fingers to linger in his for a moment longer than was necessary. *How about putting survival at the top of the agenda, buddy boy?*

When they next stopped to rest, he recounted the supplies in his pack. Three bottles of water and six food pouches. With two adults and two dogs needing constant hydration, they were going to outstrip his supplies. Fortunately, Steph would have toted along more than enough for the competition. The rain was falling and they could collect that to drink to supplement if necessary, but they'd have to stay in one place for an extended period and that was akin to painting a nice bright target on their backs.

Did Steph have a better idea? He was going to ask her when she pumped a fist in the air.

"I got a bar."

He looked up from his jumbled supplies, distracted. "Chocolate?"

"No, phone," she snapped, shoving the cell at him.

"Better than chocolate." Nerves zinging, he took a knee next to her as her fingers punched in a number. His own phone was still not showing any connection whatsoever. Why hadn't he purchased a satellite phone?

"It's ringing," she said. He scrunched

his face close to hers, hearing the phone chirp unsteadily as if it was struggling to connect them to the outside world.

Come on, little signal. Hang in there. You got this.

A woman answered. "Hello?"

He bit back a crow of triumph. Finally.

"Kara," Stephanie almost shouted. "I'm in the Lost Sierras with Vance Silverton. Ferris Grinder is here hunting us. No one knows we're—" She pulled the phone away from her ear in dismay. "It cut out."

He tried to tamp down his disappointment. "How much do you think she heard?"

"No idea. Not even sure she finished her 'hello' before it quit." Fatigue shadowed Steph's face and snuffed out what had been a joyful smile. His heart ached at her downcast expression.

"It's okay. Even if she only got one word, it could make her start to question what's going on."

She sighed. "Maybe."

He nudged her elbow with his. "Come

on, Steph. This is your sister we're talking about. When we were together, you used to tell me how hard she was working to save her chickens from being eaten by coyotes. Think how much harder she'll work to find you once she realizes something's amiss."

She didn't smile, but the corners of her mouth turned up slightly. "Yeah. The coyotes are still a problem for Kara. I've been trying to help her with a plan to protect her birds that doesn't involve her staying up with Dad's shotgun all night."

He cajoled her into eating a handful of M&M's. "Another half hour and we'll be at the rim of the valley. And the rain's holding off."

She held out her palm for more M&M's. "And we've got candy, which is better than my healthy options. Food of champions, right?"

He laughed, delighted that her spirit had revived somewhat. "Yes, ma'am." He poured some out for her and tossed a few into his mouth. Strangely, they tasted better than any he'd ever eaten before.

When she was ready, they struggled on. Undeniably, their pace was slowing. Steph had a blister on the back of her heel so she'd changed back into her regular boots, but they hadn't dried out from her plunge into the river. Her feet had to be as cold and painful as his. Pudge's fatigue made him clumsy to the point that Vance picked him up again, securing him close with the sling.

They sojourned on until they arrived at a spot to rest, just before they'd plunge down into the meadow. He freed Pudge, took out his binoculars and climbed onto a rock. Body complaining, he lay on his stomach and scanned. His watch told him it was past lunch time, but the atmosphere was gloomy and dim. They'd been trekking steadily since before sunup.

The meadow was alive with wind-rippled serpents of grass. The Jeep was parked where they'd abandoned it. There was no indication of any human presence. It might have been an eternity ago he'd encountered Steph at the first checkpoint, pinned down by gunfire, frantic to find her escort, Gina. The memory brought back pain. Gina, the feel of her hand snatched loose from his, that last look before she vanished... If he'd been quicker, more agile...

A rock poked him in the belly, bringing him back to the present. Mentally he put away the failure with Gina, shoved it into that vault where all of his worst defeats were locked away. He adjusted the lenses and continued his sweep of the valley, the trees beyond, the steep slope and the sharp drop-off that would take them out of the meadow and on their way to rescue. A blip of color caught his attention amid the muddy brown of the trees. He looked again, fingers strangling the binoculars. His mouth went dry.

"Steph," he snapped. "We've got a complication."

She immediately climbed up next to him. "More complicated than a killer with a drone?"

He handed her the binoculars. "At your eleven."

She hissed out a breath as she saw what he had. A horse, tail swishing, barely visible as the rider guided it into the trees. She groaned. "This is unbelievable."

"Your instincts were right. Evan the cowboy's a player in this game."

"He's operating the drone for Ferris?"

"I think that's what's in the black bag he's carrying."

She shook her head. "This is like some kind of ridiculous TV show. We can't catch a break."

Ferris. Two women victims. Now Evan added to the mix. The complications were stacking up and they all worked in Ferris's favor. Vance ran through their plans, searching for ways to adjust in light of the new threat.

"We can scrap the Jeep idea. Climb

higher and see if we can get another, stronger signal. Head for…"

Steph shook her head. "I'm tired, Vance. We all are. There's no way we can hike out of here. We need that Jeep."

He heard the tinge of desperation in her words. He felt twinges of it himself, though he'd walk over coals before he'd articulate that to her. "The positive in this is that Evan's heading away from us, into the trees. Ferris probably directed him to keep tabs on the Jeep in case we returned for it, but he's finished his check for now. I think he's going to use the remaining daylight hours to find a spot to hole up for the night. It'd be dangerous for him to ride in the dark in this terrain, right? We can stall, give him some time and distance to move away. Sneak into the meadow after dark. If we can't find the keys, I can hotwire it." Unless Ferris had returned and disabled this vehicle too.

"If Evan's close enough, he'll hear the

engine. Put up the drone and alert Ferris immediately."

"That will take time for him to realize what's going on and launch. All we need is five minutes to get out of the meadow. If we see any sign of the drone, we can hide the vehicle or you can shoot down the drone, if it comes to that."

"Now that would be satisfying," she admitted.

"Worst case, Ferris and Evan are immediately on to us. I know we can get to the Jeep before the horse and I'm a way better driver than Ferris, that's certain." He added a cocky grin and gave her a mock punch to the shoulder.

She grabbed his wrist, playfully, but then she laced her fingers through his. "Thanks for trying to lighten the mood, but the truth is, we don't really have many options, do we? We're not going to survive much longer on foot."

He gripped her fingers and pulled her knuckles close, kissing them.

"We're going to make it out of here, Steph."

"And you're certain because..." She leaned an inch closer, her lips near his. "Marines know things..."

"And we do stuff." Before he could re-think it, he closed the gap between them and kissed her. His brain struggled to cat-alog the feelings, the warmth, softness, a touch full of life and tenderness. All the emotions flooded and flashed their way through him like sunlight reflected off moving water. She leaned into him for the barest tic, allowing the kiss to continue, and then she sat back.

He was unsteady, unmoored.

Her breathing appeared a bit off-kilter too.

"Vance..." she began.

His spirit dropped as he heard her unspo-ken message. It wasn't what she wanted. He wasn't what she needed. "I'm sorry," he mumbled.

She stared at him, tucked the hair behind

her ear and shrugged. "It's okay. Strange times, right?"

The strangest, because the truth was, he wasn't the slightest bit sorry he'd kissed her. Unfortunately, she did not feel the same. "Yes, ma'am."

She grabbed her pack and rifled through it, her way of reinserting an appropriate distance between them. "If we're going to wait until dark, might as well eat. It's my turn to make dinner. No steak and lobster, but I'll see what I can do."

He sat quietly as she made preparations. She opened packets, poured water, accepted his propane burner.

He watched and wondered, trying to cement the memory of what was undoubtedly the last kiss he'd ever share with Stephanie Wolfe.

When the hour came for the dinner meal, she did her best, but it was not as satisfying as the oatmeal. She'd reconstituted her supply of organic beef stew, which they spooned right out of the packets. To add a flourish, she'd gone so far as to plop a dollop of it into each dog's kibble and they'd gobbled it like it was a fine filet.

Vance also appeared to enjoy the meal and it pleased her to provide it, glad it brought out the dimple in his smile, happy to feel his fingers brush hers as he accepted it. She rued her own thoughts. Vance might be comfortable entertaining notions that they could get back together again, but she wasn't.

Why not?

The thought rested like a stone in her stomach.

Why not? Because he'd hurt her. He was a man who'd consider betrayal if the stakes were high enough, his devotion to Lettie stronger than his affection for her. That's what her wounds told her anyway. Was it true?

She stiffened. And was that the real root of it? That Steph hadn't been first in his heart? Her own words poked at her.

That's God's kind of love, Vance. Honoring and respecting in spite of your feelings, not because of them. And hadn't she personally witnessed him honoring and respecting her wishes even under the extreme duress they'd been experiencing?

Her mind flashed back to a police call two winters prior, to which they'd both been dispatched. It replayed in vivid detail. An elderly lady had run into the street, hysterical after finding her husband deceased in his living-room chair. They'd been on their way home from a training event, where Vance had volunteered to be the "bad guy" and gotten roughed up by a police dog. His pants were torn at the knees and there was a smudge of dirt on his forehead. One minute they'd been discussing purchasing some steaks to grill for dinner, and the next, the lady had lurched into the street almost in front of their vehicle. Steph had slammed on the brakes and called it in while Vance ran into the house with the frenzied woman.

By the time Steph had made it into the residence to join him, Vance had guided the woman into a chair and sat next to her at a scarred kitchen table. He'd caught Stephanie's eye, given her the barest shake of his head, indicating he'd checked and there was nothing to be done for the woman's husband.

"What am I going to do?" the woman wailed, breath coming in terrified pants as she twisted the cross around her neck with arthritic fingers. "We've been married for fifty-two years. What am I going to do?"

Vance clasped her small hands inside his big ones and scrunched his tall frame to look directly into her stark face. "I'm going to stay here with you. We're going to pray together until your family comes. Would that be all right?"

She'd nodded and Steph watched in utter awe as Vance calmed the woman with sweet prayers of comfort. The moment had embedded itself deep in Steph's soul too. She had grown up a believer, but she defaulted to herself she realized, not God. Problem? She'd fix it and pray about it later.

But Vance had done the reverse in that small space of time. There wasn't anything they could have fixed. No way to alter any of the stark facts. The woman had clutched his fingers as personnel arrived to transport her husband. He'd led her into the kitchen before the medics did their job, preparing her a cup of tea to spare her witnessing the removal of the body. His entire purpose had been providing comfort and support until her son arrived. Then Vance had kissed her on the cheek and scrawled his personal cell-phone number on her notepad. "If you need anything at all, Mrs. Brubaker, you can call me anytime." And he'd meant every word.

She'd called from time to time. He'd brought her a box from his supply of Scout cookies. When she cooked pot roast he was always invited.

Steph had started to fall for him then, in

the terrified woman's kitchen—the man with the torn pants and the dirt on his forehead.

Maybe there was an answer for her tucked away somewhere in those memories that she couldn't grasp at the moment. At the very least, she could show care and respect for Vance in spite of her feelings. She didn't have to accelerate all the way to love. It certainly wasn't the time for that development. Plus, she and Vance had tried couplehood and she was wise enough now to know it wasn't going to work out. *Care and respect. Stick with that.*

And she did care, she discovered. More than she could have imagined two days before.

He leaned back against a tree trunk and stretched until his spine cracked. He was disheveled, a new hole in the elbow of his jacket. "Something wrong?"

She jerked, realizing she'd been standing like a silent lump with her empty stew packet, gazing at him. "Uh, no. I was…" She floundered until she noticed the cooling water. "I'll pour this back into the bottles. I have tablets, by the way—purification tablets, so we can collect river water and make it potable if our supplies run low." If they were stuck there much longer, water might be the least of their difficulties.

"Excellent. I didn't want to mention the water thing, but it was climbing to the top of my list." He held up his half-empty bottle and capped it carefully.

Once their bottles were full, she poured the remainder of the cooled water into the dogs' bowls and they both drank heartily.

The scant sunlight disappeared from the sky as she stowed the trash and repacked. Vance returned to his position on the rock, switching to night-vision binoculars as the valley plunged into velvety darkness.

Ten more minutes and he gave her a thumbs-up.

"No return of Cowboy Evan. Rain's

holding off. All factors trending in our favor," he reported with a goofy grin.

If that was the case, why did she have a sickening sense of foreboding?

She scanned the gloomy landscape, the Jeep nestled innocuously in the grass below like a resting beetle.

Was Ferris lurking there too? Had he already disabled the vehicle? Planned a trap?

She stroked Chloe's ears. "I know you'll tell me if Ferris is nearby, won't you, girl?"

Chloe's head was a soft pillow for Steph's cold cheek. Her siblings would have been there in an instant, if they only knew of her predicament. She prayed Kara had gotten enough of her frantic report to start investigating. But with Roman and Chase working cases, and Kara helping their mother recover from back surgery, would she be able to rally the troops quickly?

Not in time to face the upcoming challenge. One way or another, the next few hours would change everything. She looked up to find Vance watching her. Silently he reached out a hand.

She took it, and together they prayed.

EIGHT

Vance took the lead just after midnight, closing in on the Jeep in a slow crouch that made his knees crack. As he reached the point where he'd have to step out of cover, he gave Steph a raised fist to stop her progress with the dogs. A glance behind told him she'd slowed to a halt, still sheltered by the rocks. They'd argued about the plan, but there was no denying she was better at controlling the dogs than he was; smarter for her to bring up the rear. Suited him fine. He'd do the initial recon and if Ferris was hiding, ready to pounce, Steph would have a chance to either back him up or get away. He hoped she'd take off at the first sign of trouble.

Who was he kidding? She wasn't about

to turn tail and leave him to die. Love—in this case the generic type of tenderness for a fellow human—was about action, she'd told him. She would act to assist him, instead of protecting herself.

And that worried him. Deeply.

He'd cost her enough and he didn't want to contemplate her taking a bullet for him. Or anyone. The mere suggestion that she could get hurt made his stomach heave. It wasn't love, he figured, since that would be a one-sided proposition for sure. It must be that same generic-tenderness-for-a-fellow-human thing again. But he could not quite breathe away the prickly cascade of emotion he felt for Steph.

"Lord…" he whispered.

The rest of the prayer was a silent conversation. He slunk forward, leaving the brush and crawling through the grass with his gun in one hand. The movement was both awkward and painful when his knuckles, knees and elbows encountered rocks. Wind threw drizzle in his face, down his back, further dampening his already clammy jeans. The Jeep was in sight now, windows beaded with moisture on the outside but not clouded on the interior. All right. No one breathing inside. Ferris wasn't hunkered down waiting to kill them.

Encouraging. But that didn't mean Ferris hadn't left another deadly snare in place for them to find.

Steph would be scanning the wider area with binoculars while he focused solely on the vehicle. Reaching the driver's-side door, he tried the handle. Unlocked. On his feet now, he eased open the door and checked the interior, gun cocked and ready. As he'd thought. No concealed killers. A relieved sigh escaped his lips. The keys were gone, of course, but all he needed was two minutes to overcome that problem. He prayed the engine would work.

He gave Steph a signal and slithered into the driver's seat. The cold material permeated his spine. With the screwdriver from his backpack, he pried off the ignition panel and exposed the wires. A quick snip with his cutters to sever and reconnect the electrical system brought the interior lights to life. His excitement surged at the soft glow. This might actually go off without a hitch.

He darted a look to see Steph moving fast now, the two dogs racing next to her. He cut the starter wire, stripped the ends and touched them together. The engine chugged to life with a sound more beautiful than music. He tore off two pieces of tape and covered the live tips. By the time he'd finished, Steph had thrown the rear door open, loaded the dogs and flung herself into the passenger seat. Her breath puffed white clouds as she continued to do her reconnaissance job while he put the Jeep in gear and rolled it free from its grassy nest.

A moment later the wheels caught and spun in the soft earth. *Not now. Please. Not stuck. Please do not do that.* The engine noise would have alerted Ferris or Evan if they were close. They couldn't be trapped here in the mud. Five heart-stopping seconds and the Jeep pulled free. Sweat rolled down his temples. He kept the lights off, moving to the more solid ground that led to the steep grade out of the valley. He prayed they would not fall victim to any mud pits.

His elation was so great he didn't feel her tugging at his arm, peering at the dash. "Vance," she said. "There's…"

She stopped as a figure stepped into view dead center in the path in front of them.

Whatever she'd been about to say died on her lips.

Ferris strode forward as confidently as if he was going to accept an award, the rifle aimed at the front windshield. Steph gripped her gun, but firing at Ferris would require her sticking her head out the window. Same story in his case. Just what Ferris would want—two easy kill shots.

Vance stopped, engine idling. He had to turn the tables to give them a chance. Desperate measures… "Count of three, you turn on the brights, Steph."

"What? No." A vein jumped in her jaw. "Whatever you're planning, forget it."

She looked completely fierce as she stared him down—fierce and beautiful and brave and perfect. He grabbed her hand, felt her tremble. "Three," he said, throwing himself from the car as she scrambled to turn on the headlights. The dogs barked madly.

Ferris flung up an arm to shield his eyes and Vance took the precious advantage. At an oblique angle, he fired. Ferris flinched, the bullets missing him. Vance was moving too fast to aim properly, so he dove headfirst at Ferris, only managing to catch one ankle. Ferris sidestepped and kicked at him, connecting with Vance's chin as he scuttled backward.

White-hot pain almost immobilized Vance but he rolled and staggered to his feet, weapon still clutched in his fist. Ferris did the same, ready to fire. Rifle versus revolver. Two men determined to get off the lethal shot.

"There's no way you're going to survive this," Ferris said.

"Funny, I had the same thought about you."

Ferris cocked his head. "You keep on persisting in the face of inevitable failure. It's refreshing. Honestly I thought you'd both crumble without your badges and reinforcements. It's been more satisfying than I'd imagined, this plan of mine."

Sweat trickled from his throbbing forehead. Where was Steph? Still in the Jeep? "We're scrappy."

Ferris smiled. "So here we are, both armed and dangerous. Like a standoff in the Old West. You can almost hear the tumbleweeds rolling along. Dad and I loved watching those old black and white movies."

Vance's palms were slick with sweat as

he gripped the gun, trying to visualize the possibilities. If Ferris fired, it could easily penetrate the Jeep. If Vance fired, he'd have one chance to immobilize Ferris, who had the Kevlar advantage on his side. Unlikely he'd succeed. There had to be a better way.

"The difference between you and me is," Ferris said, a smile spreading, "I brought backup."

The cowboy stepped from the bushes holding a long-bladed knife. Enemies doubled.

Vance caught the sound, the barest tap on the accelerator, Steph's warning to him. He chuckled. "Would you look at that? Looks like I did too."

As the Jeep plowed forward, Ferris and Evan dove into the grass. Vance barely managed to avoid being run over. He executed a clumsy tumbling roll that knocked the wind out of him. Somehow, he regained his footing as the Jeep showered him with debris. The closest door was the driver side and he leaped in, Steph scooting over. Ferris and Evan were upright now too.

He punched the gas. The Jeep rattled and rumbled over the ground. "Stay down," he yelled at her. There was no way to keep clear of the men with the trees and jagged rocks on either side.

He caught one quick glimpse of Ferris as they zoomed past.

Smiling? Why not shooting? Maybe he'd been hurt trying to avoid Steph's onslaught.

Rocks zinged from under the tires and he prayed they didn't have a blowout. The grade was steep, but the sturdy vehicle took it well. The dogs were bunched together on the back seat. Pudge whined as the wheels bounced and they slid to the other side.

"I can't believe you did that." Steph twisted to track Ferris out the back window. Her anger was palpable.

"There was no other way."

"Running him down with us both safe in the Jeep might have been an option," she snapped.

"Not with his rifle skills, and I might point out you took a risk there too. You almost flattened me."

"No chance of that with your catlike reflexes."

"Not the time for sarcasm, ma'am."

She braced herself against the door. "Why didn't he shoot us when we went for the Jeep in the first place?"

"He's enjoying himself too much." He kept to the middle of the narrow path, but the vehicle was still wide enough to take out branches on both sides. "He's trying to see how much torture he can apply before he ends us."

"Vance..."

"Hold that thought for a minute, okay?" He was forced to slow as the steep slope gave way to a perilous drop that made the dogs whine and his own stomach lurch. After getting up and over the peak, the

Jeep was tipped, nose down, until he was practically standing on the brakes. "Couple more yards and it bottoms out again," he said through gritted teeth. "There's another area of grassland ahead, which leaves us exposed but we'll punch our speed as much as we can. Unlikely he can take us out while we're moving. More cover after that with the trees."

"I don't think so. There's…"

He gripped the wheel as the Jeep slammed up and over a fallen branch he hadn't seen. "We can either make for the competition finish line, where there will likely be people around, or the main road, whichever comes first."

She slapped a palm on her thigh. "Neither one of those is gonna work, Silverton."

What was that tone for? Now he was getting miffed. "Just because you're mad about my methods doesn't mean the plan is bad."

"It's not going to work," she insisted, stabbing a finger at the dashboard display.

"What?"

She directed him to the gas gauge. "Look."

He flat-out gaped.

"That's what I've been trying to tell you." Steph's tone flattened from angry to discouraged. "Chloe alerted just before we got in. Ever since the courthouse she can sense when Ferris comes into our proximity. She detected that he'd been around the Jeep sometime recently and she let me know. She was right."

He could hardly make his eyes believe what he was seeing. They'd come so far, risked so much. But the little red needle pointing to E was undeniable. They were nearly out of fuel.

She heaved out a breath. "Ferris out-guessed us, figured we would head for a working vehicle since he disabled mine, yours and Elizabeth's. He siphoned the gas. We're going to stall out in open coun-

try and he knows it. Just his way of pro-
longing the game. Like you said, he's
enjoying it too much."

Vance stared.

The needle fluttered even lower.

Ferris had indeed outguessed them. They
were outguessed, outgunned and running
out of time.

He pushed the Jeep, gas pedal to the
floor, but it was only gravity pulling them
along now. The trees thinned out around
them, the sparse canopy allowing the rain
to hammer the roof as the engine began
to sputter.

A howl of rage built inside him.

Ferris had won again.

Steph had her backpack on before the
motor completely fizzled. The dogs needed
no command to exit the car. They sensed
the urgency and catapulted free as soon
as she opened the door for them. Pudge
immediately looked around to find some
avenue to escape the pounding rain.

Vance recovered from his shock enough to quickly search the Jeep for anything useful that might aid their survival. Steph was too numb and disappointed to help him. She couldn't imagine what would make their current situation easier and Ferris had probably stripped out anything that might be of use anyway. Ferris had wanted them to experience hope so he could rip it away.

Vance was an optimist though, even now. She felt no such emotion. They were in deep trouble and it was only getting worse. Ferris would double back to his own vehicle, hers maybe, and pursue them, relishing every moment, no doubt. Worse yet he had Evan on horseback to track them too and she'd seen the knife so Evan wasn't merely a spy. He'd kill them if Ferris gave him the command. They'd seen his face and could testify as to his role in the murder plot. She spared one precious moment before they ran to the trees to glance at her phone. No signal.

He reached the sheltering branches a moment after she did.

"The Jeep plan went up in smoke. Now what? River or mountain?" he demanded.

She blinked away her stupor and tried to focus. Their two options were ominous. The Feather River thundered nearby, funneling off the high mountain peaks of the northern Sierra Nevada. The river's main forks and offshoots snaked through precarious canyons, with Class 3, 4 and 5 rapids made worse recently by a historic spring snowmelt. Unlikely they'd find any kayakers in the wild waters to help them, not at this time of year, and not in a nasty storm.

She cast a look at the stern granite peak rising above the trees. Climbing would be arduous, impossible even. They'd never reach the other side, but the choice held the hope they might encounter a rough weather hiker or an empty campground where they could find shelter and a possible signal. Most significantly, Ferris would assume they'd follow the waterway, which would lead them to one of the tiny towns dotted here and there throughout the Lost Sierra. He'd be sure to complete his executions before they set foot in any of them.

"Mountain," she said, explaining her reasoning. "Unless you have another idea."

"Not at the moment." He rubbed a bump on his forehead. "My last plan wasn't worth much, was it?"

"I didn't see it coming either." His demeanor was different, worrying her. "You all right?"

He waved off her question. "Ready, dogs?"

Pudge and Chloe both wagged their tails. Vance took the lead position.

She figured they didn't have long before Ferris regrouped. Evan would send up a drone to search the meadow, the trails. Though it was still far from sunrise, it was possible the drone had low light tracking capabilities. At least the bits of granite and leaves covering the ground would conceal their footprints. Maybe the violent rainfall would make it harder for the drone to spy on them. They would need any slim advantage to survive long enough to get help.

She moved as fast as she could, keeping up with Vance's quick pace in spite of the growing agony in her feet. The gush of warmth indicated her heels were bloody, but there was no question about stopping to treat her wounds. She could hear her wild brother Chase's slogan echoing in her brain. "Pain is never permanent," he'd said while recovering from the various injuries he'd sustained as an Army Scout and his often reckless behavior in his leisure time.

And it wasn't going to be permanent now. She straightened and pushed on.

Vance tripped once, catching himself. His gait was less fluid than normal. Had he suffered a head injury tackling Ferris? Or was it merely fatigue and the uneven trail? She suggested a moment of rest, but he declined.

Chloe stayed by her side, vaulting over rocks and fallen logs. Steph was thankful she kept up Chloe's exercise regimen regardless of the season. Pudge maintained a better pace than she'd thought possible. He'd need to be carried eventually…if they survived long enough. If Vance was too tired, she could lug him for a while, maybe borrow the sling. He was such an ungainly dog, the opposite of her beautiful bloodhound, but he was a loyal, dedicated soul who was quickly taking up a big spot in her heart. The guilt she felt about ensnaring Chloe into their perilous situation must be something Vance was grappling with too with his dog. What would happen to Pudge if and when they got back to civilization? Vance had a tiny apartment with a no-pet policy.

She was encouraged when they stumbled upon a mile marker almost covered by overgrowth. "We're on an official trail of some sort, thankfully." When she unfurled the map to check, Vance bent over to shield her and the flapping paper from the driving rain.

"Yes, here it is," she said. "It leads…"

Vance shushed her and they went still. He pulled her into the crook of his arm. She could feel his heart thud against her shoulder. The drone zoomed above them, its metallic eye searching. She pressed her face to his chest.

"I'd give a week's pay to shoot that thing down," Vance muttered.

"Same."

He kept her close and for a moment she forgot the circling drone and the pain in her heels and the hunger and bone-deep fatigue. There was comfort in his touch, the way he held her close enough to protect her, but gently too. He'd treated her throughout their ordeal with enough respect to communicate that he valued who she was, and what she thought, and the decisions she made. Every breath he took encouraged her to relax against him. So comfortable, she thought. So right.

You're reading into this, Steph. Running for your life isn't helping your mental state. But she absorbed the warmth anyway while the moments ticked by, as if she was powerless to separate herself. They remained motionless until the drone moved off to search another area.

She bit her lip as they stepped apart, covering her jumbled emotions by sipping water and offering some to the dogs along with a jerky snack. Ahead was a crooked switchback that appeared to lead straight up at a merciless pitch. Vance slumped as he perused their path.

He had something to say, something important. She waited.

"Steph, even with the drone gone, we're in a dog's breakfast here."

One of Vance's favorite expressions when they were on the force together. A dog's breakfast was the remains of whatever the chef had ruined and made unfit for human consumption. She didn't like the flatness of his tone, the rounding of his impossibly wide shoulders.

"Speak for yourself," she said lightly. "My dog eats the finest quality breakfast."

Her joke didn't work. He faced her with hands on hips.

"I think we should separate."

She recoiled. "What?"

"I'll move away, draw them off, divert them long enough that you can find someone to help, or at least hide. You've got rations and I'll give you mine too. That will allow you a couple more days."

She folded her arms, scared but determined to firmly and calmly talk him out of his notion. "No. We're not doing that."

"Steph, we're running out of options and time."

The bruise on his cheekbone was dark purple and she noticed dried blood in his hairline.

His mouth was set, brow furrowed. If he decided the best way to save her was sacrificing himself, she wouldn't be able to change his mind, so she let her instincts take over. She lifted her hands to his cheeks, thumbs brushing his lips.

He put a palm over hers, eyes closed as he cupped her hand to his face.

"Listen to me," she said softly.

He didn't look at her so she pressed her forehead to his. "Vance? I need you to hear me."

He leaned back slightly and opened his eyes.

She maintained their connection. "The only reason we're still alive is that we've stuck together."

He grimaced. "I should have sent the cops in the first place, not gone after Ferris myself. Insisted you quit the competition."

"The cops have other things to do besides chasing people who skip out on parole." She gently eased up his chin until she was looking into his eyes. She remembered the soft green, the color of rain-soaked spring leaves. "And regarding your idea that you should have forced me to quit the competition, when was the last time you were able to force me to do anything I didn't want to do?"

His fingers tightened on hers. "He's already killed two women. I—"

"Vance." She pulled their joined hands to her and squeezed tight until he stopped talking, willing him to listen and accept, praying he would not leave her. "We're partners again right now, like we were back on the force. Partners don't abandon each other. Ever."

He stared at her, drew her hand to his lips, pressed his cold chin against her skin. Her heart fluttered as he kissed her knuckles one at a time. "I can't bear it if you get hurt," he said softly. "I've taken a lot in my life, but I cannot survive that. I won't survive it."

The words were so precious, considering. She'd been hurt, deeply wounded by this man, but love was action and he surely was behaving as if he loved her still. Or maybe again? Could they be discovering each other in a new way?

She forced a smile. "Improvise, adapt and overcome, isn't that what you Marines say?"

He blinked.

"Didn't think I'd remember?" she asked.

"Didn't think you listened."

"I listened to every word you ever said to me." Every word, every nuance, every look had been written on the pages of her mind until the book had slammed shut between them. Shut for always.

Without warning, he scooped her in an embrace and rested his chin on her head. "I dreamed of reconnecting with you over and over, but not this way."

Dreamed of reconnecting? She felt the pressure of his hug, the breadth of the muscled shoulders that had made him a champion swimmer in college. But that's all this was, a surreal dream. Nothing real existed between her and Vance outside this nightmarish bubble. Did it?

She and Vance were partners for the moment. And running through the Lost Sierra an inch away from a killer hadn't changed anything.

Survival.

That was all they had to worry about.

Survival, and making sure Ferris got the punishment he deserved.

She pulled away from him and he let her go. "We stick together. Period."

With a sigh, he took off his cap, wiped his brow and gestured with it. "All right then. Ladies first."

She could not restrain a giggle as she forced her body into motion.

"What's so funny?"

"Your cap. You still write your passwords inside your hat because you can't remember them."

He rolled his eyes. "I remembered them just fine when I had the same one for everything."

"Getmeasandwichasap?" she asked as

she skirted a puddle the size of a man-hole cover.

"Yeah, that one, until it got hacked and you made me promise not to use the same passwords for everything." He slapped at a low branch. "Letters, numbers, symbols, uppercase and lower? Who can remember all that? I'm not into codes and stuff. What can I say?"

So true. His motto was I Don't Math in Public. Again he reached to clear a branch, this one low-lying, to assist Pudge.

"What are you going to do with Pudge when the case is over?" she asked.

He frowned. "What do you mean?"

"Are you going to return him?"

The look he tossed her was pure disgust. "You actually think I'd dump him back in the shelter? Are you kidding me?" Vance glared at her and covered Pudge's ears. "Don't let him hear you say a thing like that. You think I'd discard him like some sort of ugly sweater?" he whispered. "I hope he didn't hear you. He's sensitive."

She was struck silent with a combination of amusement and awe. "You're keeping him?"

He uncovered the dog's ears. "Well, of course I'm keeping him. Good grief, Steph. You've accused me of lots of terrible things but that's got to be the worst."

"I apologize."

He blew out a breath, clearly still offended. "I understand I broke your trust and you figure I'm a scoundrel, but I promise you I would never dump Pudge. He was in the shelter next to a kind of intense roommate like I told you about. Hence, Pudge stayed in the corner. When I showed up, he waddled over and pressed himself to the bars with these pleading eyes, as if he was saying 'Please take me home and we can be best friends forever.' How could I walk away from that?" He bent and kissed the dog's fat wedge of a head. "You're Daddy's Pudgy, aren't you? We're friends for life, right?"

She tried to take in the sight of the big

man who'd broken her heart, crooning baby talk to an overweight mutt as if the animal was a precious infant.

Pudge happily slurped a tongue over Vance's nose. "I guess I got us both into a lot of trouble here, didn't I?" Vance said. He locked eyes with Steph. "I should have tried harder to contact you before the event, tell you what I was up to."

Something inside her loosened. "And I should have listened to you when you showed up at the start line."

"I'm sorry," they both said at once. Pudge lathered Vance with another dog kiss.

"But you can't keep him at your apartment, can you?" she asked.

"No, but I didn't like that place anyway. Terrible parking and the air conditioner isn't up to snuff. And those weird curtains were never my style. Who puts roosters on curtains? We've been staying in pet-friendly hotels while tracking Ferris, but when I get back, he'll bunk with Aunt

Lettie while I pack up the apartment." He arched an eyebrow at her. "Pudgy is mine now. Forever." He stalked farther ahead, obviously still miffed at her.

And you misjudged him. Maybe it was better to have him annoyed with her than trying to start up a relationship again. Grateful that at least she'd rekindled a fire in him, she smiled in spite of her discomfort as her new view of Vance settled into her soul.

Vance wouldn't let Pudge down and he wouldn't let her down either. Not again. He'd fight to the last breath, the final moment. He was brave enough to stay the course, strong enough to apologize for what he'd done wrong.

Her heart was still fluttering at an accelerated rate from their physical connection. What in the world? She had to be suffering from dehydration or stress or low electrolytes to be imagining things about Vance, a delirium born of danger. Any moment the drone could pinpoint their location again. Ferris's rifle shot might find them from behind a rock or tree, no matter how fast they pushed on.

How were they going to escape?

Friday morning was nearly upon them. The weather was worsening. The chances that they'd run into anyone who could help them was slim to nonexistent.

If they could only get a signal...

Her phone was juiced up thanks to her solar charger.

One text or call and the whole game would change.

Just keep moving, Steph.

But she could feel her body weakening. Vance was slowing too and she'd barely talked him out of separating.

Did they have enough stamina to outlast Ferris Grinder and company?

Soon their physical state would leave them at his mercy, no matter how great their determination.

NINE

They'd been hiking the whole day along a ragged trail which Steph was sure would connect to a bigger path in the space of twelve miles. Twelve miles might as well be a thousand, he thought. On the plus side, there had been no further drone sightings and the way they were going would make it unlikely Ferris could follow in a vehicle. But the minuses still overshadowed the pluses. Vance had been carrying Pudge for the last mile and he'd stumbled so many times he feared he'd drop the dog. Areas of thick mud forced them to stop and chew up time going around. The day elapsed in painful increments until finally the sun was low in the sky. Vance's nerves began to prickle as the daylight disappeared behind the mountain peaks.

Even Chloe was lagging, though they'd stopped regularly. The competition allowed only for daytime participation, since the terrain was rugged. Smart rule. Marching around in the dark and cold was stressful and hazardous, especially without the prescribed rest hours in a nice, watertight tent. At least they had enough supplies, though he probably hadn't packed enough of something.

When Steph tripped and went to one knee, he hurried to give her a hand up, and she leaned heavily on him. Chloe slurped an anxious tongue across Steph's cheek, but it was clear the dog was depleted too.

"We gotta camp until morning. Rest and refuel." He figured she'd argue but she didn't. Telling.

"Where?" was all she said.

"I'll find a spot—and you're gonna love this part." He yanked the slender bundles

208 *Hunted on the Trail*

from his pack. "Two ultralight sleeping bags I swiped from the Jeep."

Her eyes lit in a way that made his breath hitch. "Really?" she squeaked. "Ferris left them there?"

"They were stowed behind the seats. I think it was meant as extra competition gear. Or Ferris is simply making things more sporting. Anyway I figure a human and a dog per bag and that's gonna be tight, but warm. We can lay them over there, down in the hollow. Don't think a drone can get close with all those branches and fortunately they're black so they will be even less visible. What do you say? I can even toss in a meal to sweeten the offer."

"Perfection."

Pleased with himself, he enjoyed a spurt of energy as they hurried to the small depression in the ground. Thick pines added a carpet of needles. Together they spread out the bags and arranged their makeshift camp.

"Food or sleep first?"

"I'm too tired to eat," Steph said.

"Sleep it is. It's almost five o'clock," he said. "We'll overnight here, aim to move out again at three a.m. I'll take the first shift while you sleep."

She crawled into the sleeping bag and held the side open so Chloe could burrow in next to her. Pudge tried to join them.

"You got your own bag, buddy." He unzipped his and smoothed it out a few feet from Steph and Chloe. Pudge slithered inside down to the bottom.

Steph wriggled a few times until she and Chloe reached some sort of comfortable compromise. Something missing, he thought. The sling would do. He folded it into a small rectangle and kneeled next to her.

"Use this for a pillow."

She lifted her head and he slid it under her cheek. And because he was tired, or out of his mind, or maybe just too uncomfortable to deny his craving, he bent down and kissed her on the lips. "Sleep well, Steph."

She smiled as her eyes closed.

Vance returned to his sleeping bag and sat atop it, away from the lump of Pudge, back against the tree. He checked his gun and laid it next to him.

"Vance?" Steph's voice was small and delicate in the great big emptiness.

"Yes?"

"You promise you won't leave me?"

That tiny little-girl voice coming from that strong-as-a-lion woman made a lump form in his throat. How could he put his ferocious surge of emotion into words? He swallowed hard. "No, honey. I will not leave you. I promise."

And he wouldn't. Not until there was no breath left in him, or worse, until she asked him to. It wasn't until that very moment that he understood how big and deep and wide were his feelings for Stephanie Wolfe. "Get some rest, Steph," he whispered.

When he heard the sound of her regular breathing, he committed some time to prayer. The only way they'd get out alive was with God's intervention. As much as it pained him to admit it, he was weakened, failing by the hour, and Ferris had outwitted him at every turn. He tried to settle his spine against the rough tree trunk. No matter how he squirmed, some sharp bit dug into his back.

Maybe the pain would help him fight off the sleepiness.

Because Ferris wasn't sitting back for a snooze.

He had no doubt about that.

No doubt at all.

Vance lurched awake, reaching for his weapon and his senses. His eyes were gritty, his limbs stiff and cold, as he processed the misty air all around him, the black outline of trees, the branches crackling overhead. They'd been exchanging watch duty and currently he was sup-

posed to be on, according to the sched-
ule. He threw off what was covering him
and found he was still lying on top of his
bag with Pudge burrowed at the bottom,
snoring softly. He rubbed a hand over his
foggy eyes and heaved himself to a standing position.

Steph came into focus a few feet away,
kneeling next to his propane burner. Chloe
watched the proceedings, droopy head on
her tidy paws.

Steph snagged a look at him. "Hi."

He exhaled in relief that she and Chloe
were okay in spite of his failure to keep
watch. "What time is it?"

"Almost three."

"Why didn't you alert me for my shift?"

"You were sleeping so soundly I couldn't
bear to wake you. It got really cold, so I
covered you with my bag."

His cheeks burned with mortification.
"Sorry."

"Don't be."

"Can't believe I did that. I'm awake now if you want to get some more shut-eye."

She tucked a section of hair behind her ears to better watch the burner. "We're okay. Unbelievable how rest can bring a person back to life."

He wasn't sure he'd qualify himself as fully in the living category, since his back was aching and muscles all over his body twanged like banjo strings, but he definitely felt a good deal better. More alert. Pudge squirmed up the length of the bag and shoved his head out.

"Hey, buddy. All rested up?"

Pudge wriggled free and snuggled against Vance's shins, then accepted a good ear rubbing before he went to inspect Chloe.

Vance sniffed. "Does my nose deceive me or is that the incomparable smell of oatmeal?"

She giggled. "I helped myself to your pack. Hope you don't mind."

He pointed at a smear of chocolate on

her lip, visible in the tiny glow of the burner. "I see. Sampling the ingredients too?"

Now it was her turn to blush. "They might go bad if we don't eat them."

"Of course. It was only prudent. Back in a minute." He went into the woods, where he made a quick stop and then located the small stream he'd heard nearby during his night watch. He splashed his face and hands with water so frigid it made his molars throb. How long would a person survive if submerged at that temperature? Not long. He pictured Gina for a moment before he shut off the thought and tried to squeeze the feeling into his fingers.

When he returned, the dogs were munching kibble mixed with a dribble of oatmeal and each had a container of fresh water.

"I got some from the stream and purified it," Steph said. "Refilled our water bottles."

"I missed a lot while I was conked out." He took the warm mug of oatmeal and rolled it between his cold palms, inhaling the steam as if he could feed on the vapors themselves. Warmth was a thing he'd completely taken for granted in his normal day-to-day. He never would again. "Only a few candies for me," he said. He wanted to be sure there would be enough left for her to snack on. She sprinkled in a half dozen.

After a prayer, they spooned up the hot oatmeal, illuminated by Steph's tiny penlight, which she was careful to keep partially covered. Their breath steamed the air, the clinking of their spoons mingling with the trill of some distant insect. The air was incredibly pure; the stars that peeped through the clouds shone bright as gemstones. His taste buds sang with the most intense appreciation of the humble meal. How could his senses feel so alive, more than they ever had before, when he and Steph were so close to dying?

And why, oh, why did he want to do nothing but sit in that miserable place and stare at her? Check that. He wanted to get her somewhere warm and safe and settled...where he could look and listen and laugh. With her.

He blinked, realizing she'd asked him a question.

"Come again?"

She inclined her chin at him. "I was saying I want to hike that way. There's a clearing and maybe I can snag a signal. What do you think?"

He nodded, still lost in the pleasure of the warm oatmeal hitting his famished stomach. His grin grew wider.

"Why the grin?"

"I was thinking three days ago you'd have rather shoved me aside than asked my opinion of anything."

"Three days was a lifetime ago."

He agreed.

"It's a fairly clear path so I can go check for the signal before we decamp."

She was back to her all-business approach. He should be too, except he was thinking about kissing her, the softness of her lips and the way they fit against his so perfectly.

Steph suddenly became intent on examining the sky. "I—I hope you don't... When I asked you not to leave me last night, I was tired, and exhausted, not my usual self. You understand, right?"

"Yes, we were both at the end of our ropes."

She relaxed, relieved.

"But to be clear, I told you I wouldn't and I won't." *Please tell me that's what you still want.* He watched her eyes, shifting in every direction except toward him. His spirit lagged when the moments ticked by. So it had been fatigue or fear that caused her to want him near. *Desperate times...*

She sprinkled some dog treats on the

ground. He followed suit and Chloe and Pudge gobbled them up.

She picked up the cups. "I'll wash them in the stream."

"I'll go with you."

"No need. I got it. Give me yours and I'll do both while you deal with the campsite."

He got the message and handed it over. *Pack up and stay clear.* Not surprising, her attitude, but it disappointed him anyway. Hadn't they bonded over what they'd survived? And hadn't he sensed a certain reciprocal enthusiasm in their kiss? Obviously not. Self-delusion or pride. But she was right, likely. If they were going to survive, their attention had to be on the mission, not some flighty romantic notions he'd dreamed up. *Simmer down, heart. Brain's in charge now.*

He rolled the sleeping bags and placed them into his pack again. Everything was stowed in neat, military fashion when she returned. He shouldered his pack and helped her shrug into hers, though she appeared a little squirmy from the gesture.

Manners. He could show her that much, couldn't he? Though there was undoubtedly another storm wave approaching, there was no rain at the moment. Fortunate, because the trail was murky without the benefit of daylight. The route she'd selected took them from their sheltered glen up and over a peak and onto a higher area of forest, where the trees were spaced wider apart, like gap teeth protruding from a bed of soggy, pine-needle-covered gums.

Steph had her phone out, waving it this way and that. He didn't see much sense in doing the same, but it wouldn't hurt to ascertain if he could snag a precious signal with his phone. He was digging in his pocket when he heard her gasp.

"No way," she said.

Not a signal, her expression indicated. Nothing but bad news loading. The dogs confirmed it with their rigid attention before he detected the low whir of a motor. Out of the fog emerged their old mechanical foe, the drone.

It dipped low and flittered under the canopy, yards from their location. Evan had found them. Again.

He felt his self-control snap like a flag in a freshening wind. No more would he hide like a cowering rabbit. "That's it," he growled. "I'm done."

"Vance," Stephanie hissed. "What are you doing?"

He bent to lock gazes with her. "I am tired of hiding from this drone. I won't if you tell me to stop, but I want to flip the script here. What do you say?" She'd know what he was really asking. Did she trust him?

The moment lingered and he held his breath.

When he thought she would put an end to his plans, reveal her distrust of him and widen the crack in his heart, she stepped back. Her small nod told him everything, flushed him with pride and purpose. She was entrusting her life and future to him. He would not let her down.

Blood on fire, he strode out of concealment.

Enough was enough.

The moment of truth.

Steph almost changed her mind as Vance strode past, stooping to pick up a stout branch that had fallen from the oak tree that towered above them. Her mouth went dry. She trusted him, in spite of everything, but he couldn't possibly be planning to… "Vance…"

He wasn't listening as he raced up on the flying contraption. The drone swiveled to face him, camera glinting, Evan remotely collecting every detail. She watched the unbelievable scenario play out in front of her like a scene from a movie. Vance took a warm-up swing with the branch, as a batter would behind the plate, and then arced it at the drone.

The branch smashed into the object with an impact that sent it spinning in a wobbly orbit. He'd actually hit it, wounded the thing. Pudge barked, but Vance wasn't done.

"Come here, you dirty spying robot." Another smash from Vance's makeshift weapon and it plummeted to the ground in a swirl of blinking lights.

"That's what I'm talking about," Vance crowed, taking in the drone buzzing feebly in the dirt. He rushed over and crushed the heel of his boot into the metal body, smashing it flat and sending bits of plastic and a screw flying. Pudge barked again, but Steph kept him still, hardly able to believe what she'd witnessed.

When it was over, he stood panting, hands on hips, staring down at his vanquished foe.

"That," he said after an exhale, "was deeply satisfying."

She wasn't sure whether to laugh or scream. "Effective, but you gave away our location. Even if we get out of here double time he can pinpoint our general vicinity."

Vance didn't seem at all regretful. He nudged the drone with his foot before he bent to extract a big chunk. "Changing the game. Sorry. I should have told you the entire plan before I went all Babe Ruth, but I think I had what Aunt Lettie would describe as a 'red moment.' In any case, I'm tired of playing defense and you are too. Am I right?"

"Yes." She was still bemused as he handed her the hunk of drone.

"All right then. Let's put your champion dog to work."

Now she understood, and a smile crept over her face. *Adapt, improvise, overcome...* Evan had to be within a 400-meter radius to operate the drone. "We'll have to move fast since he's on horseback."

"Copy that."

She kneeled and gave Chloe a whiff of the broken piece. No doubt Evan's scent was all over it. Chloe's nostrils quivered

as she went over every inch of the man-
gled instrument.

Stephanie shot a look at Vance while
Chloe worked. "Pretty pleased with yourself, aren't you?"

He shrugged, but his grin was not at all
modest. "Would have been a home run in
any ballpark in America. I should have
gone pro."

She laughed. "I agree. Nice piece of hitting."

"I know."

Their laughter mingled and she felt a
fresh wave of excitement and hope.

He'd just changed the game, all right,
and he hadn't discussed the details with
her beforehand, but they both knew they
couldn't continue on much longer being
hunted by two armed men. Offense was
a lot more her style, and now they would
take out the accomplice. Wouldn't be easy.
Evan had a knife and a horse and direct
communication with Ferris.

All right, God. We're gonna need a lot of help with this next part. It felt good to ask.

Chloe sat, the signal that she was done with her examination. Vance slid the piece of drone into a plastic bag she gave him in case Chloe needed a refresher.

Vance stomped the remnants of the drone a few more times. "On general principle," he said. "It's probably got a GPS tracker in there somewhere that may be functioning, so we'll leave the corpse. It would spoil our surprise attack if Evan knew we were coming."

Steph patted Chloe and cupped her fleshy chin. Everything depended on her dog's extraordinary tracking skills. Yes, she trusted Vance and she trusted Chloe too. "Ready, Chloe?"

Chloe wagged her tail.

"Find."

TEN

She clipped the long lead on Chloe to prevent her from unexpectedly encountering Evan and his knife. Chloe could perform all manner of duties, but she was completely clueless about friends and enemies. In fact, Ferris was the only person she'd ever reacted to negatively and with him it was a visceral hostility she'd never witnessed in the dog before. Everyone else they encountered was simply a collection of interesting scents that hadn't yet been sniffed out, or a potential source of treats or scratches. She wouldn't know Evan had a knife and was working with a killer.

Chloe dragged hard, urging Steph along a minuscule path with bushes on either side that clawed at her pant legs. She could see where the clusters of tall grass had been slightly flattened about halfway up the length of the stalks, probably the work of Evan's horse. Pudge yelped when he stepped on something sharp. Vance finally picked him up, earning a massive tongue slurp. He didn't put the dog in the sling, instead draping him over his shoulders like the world's weirdest cape.

She knew the reason. The sling would impede Vance's reach and he wanted to be able to pull his revolver when they found Evan. And it was definitely a "when," not an "if." Chloe was barreling onward in a familiar manner that told Steph she was latched on to a strong scent. When the dog zinged westward along a slightly more trampled path, she paused momentarily to nose at a hoofprint in the muddy margin. Steph pointed it out to Vance. He gave her a silent thumbs-up.

Confirmation. Soon now.

There was no way to keep a ninety-pound dog moving through the brush completely in stealth mode, but she hoped the brisk wind churning the leaves would muffle their progress. Chloe strained harder, yanking Steph and sparking pain all the way from her wrist to her spine. Her shoulder ached from sleeping on the ground and diving for cover every time the drone showed up. She wound the leather leash tighter around her hand. If she lost her grip now, Chloe would continue on like an out-of-control locomotive, heedless of anything but securing her prize.

The trail took them toward a grove of trees. As they drew close, she saw Chloe's body tense in that way that meant she was closing in on her target. Steph's breath caught. With enormous effort, she slowed the dog and gave Vance a fist to stop him. She pointed.

A horse cropped at a patch of soggy grass, the reins tucked loosely over the saddle horn. Steph hauled Chloe to a full stop and commanded her to sit under the shelter of a sprawling wild blackberry shrub. Vance plopped Pudge next to her. Chloe was trembling with excitement and Pudge immediately snuggled close. The horse eyed them uninterestedly and continued drifting for the next patch of lush grass to nibble.

Vance rolled his shoulders. "Showtime?"

"Yes. Evan's in there, no question."

"Then we should have our meet-and-greet." His tone was light, but his eyes shone with a simmering rage. Or perhaps it was determination. They pulled their weapons and crept slowly forward, edging past rocks and fallen trees until they could get a view of the woods.

At the same moment, they froze.

In a small circle of relatively dry pine needles, Evan was tapping at his phone, squinting at the screen, moving right and left, then tapping some more. His grizzled eyebrows were drawn together and he muttered too low for them to hear.

Vance murmured in her ear. "Flanking

from the rear. Give me thirty." Before she could argue, he'd snuck off.

Thirty seconds until everything would change one way or the other.

There had been a few events in her life where circumstances had changed in a matter of moments.

Breaking her leg during a high-school track meet...

The death of her father...

Quitting the force...

And now a showdown in the wilderness with a man she'd thought was out of her life.

Twenty-nine, twenty-eight...

She rechecked her gun. Her hands shook slightly. Fatigue, stress, exposure—all those factors would work against her shooting accuracy. Would she be sharp enough to handle the situation? A year and a half away from the force added to the rust, but she'd kept her skills sharp at the range. *Get real, Steph.* Who was she kidding? A neat, stable, shooting-range target was a completely different beast to a living, breathing enemy. And there was Vance to consider. She could not risk injuring him. There would be poor visibility in these cruel morning hours with the mist and the chill and the wind. Add in the adrenaline that was swamping her senses... So easy to make an error. A round from her gun flying at 27,000 feet per second cutting through Vance... The thought made her body go clammy.

Fifteen, fourteen...

She didn't want to shoot anyone. She prayed the next few minutes would not require her to discharge her weapon. Evan might give up without resisting. Then again, she'd seen his knife. *Vance, please be careful. We have to get out of this alive, all of us.*

All of us. When exactly had they become a pseudo family in her mind? She couldn't say, but it was undeniable. They were a unit, the four of them, which was both a terrifying and comforting feeling.

Ten, nine...

The remaining seconds evaporated.

Mouth dry as powder, she edged forward and stepped into view.

"Hands up, Evan."

Evan jerked, dropped his phone and went for his pocket, but Vance appeared and took the legs out from under the man with a quick sweep of his ankle. Evan went down on his stomach and Vance pounced on him.

Her pulse was roaring as she edged closer, tightly gripping the gun while Vance pinned Evan with his weight. She expected their prisoner to resist, but after a few vigorous thrashes, he went still.

Vance pulled Evan's hands behind his back. "Hey, Ev. 'Bout time we had a face-to-face, right? Got a moment to talk or are you too busy trying to explain to your boss how your toy got busted?"

Evan's eyes rolled. "Get off. You're suffocating me."

Vance eased up on Evan's back, but only slightly.

Stephanie moved closer and tossed Vance a set of zip ties.

He caught them with one hand. "Why do you travel around with zip ties?"

She sniffed. "They're useful, as you can plainly see." Steph noted the horse had trotted off at the tumult. The dogs were still stationary, but whining.

Vance guided Evan into a sitting position and secured his wrists. "So, Ev, how did a nice fellow like you get involved with a guy like Ferris Grinder?"

Evan scowled. "Why should I tell you?"

"So that when we get word to law enforcement, we remember exactly where we left you," Vance snapped.

Evan blanched. "Left me? Come on. You're not going to do that." His tone was not as defiant as it had been a moment before.

"Ticktock, Ev," Vance said. "Gonna start storming again soon and my dog doesn't like thunder and lightning. We gotta move out. Start talking and make it snappy. How'd you get involved with Ferris?"

Evan shrugged. "Not like we're long-time buddies or anything. Didn't even know the guy before last week. He drove by my place when I was tending my horse. Got a cabin about an hour from here. He said he was looking for someone to help him with an easy project." Evan eyed Vance and Steph. "I could use the money, so I said sure. All I had to do was volunteer to pretend to help with some dog competition and then sneak off to fly the drone and track you two."

Vance's chin went up.

Evan continued. "He showed me how to use the drone. Just like flying a model airplane, more or less."

"Except that you were using it to track us, knowing full well Ferris had murder on his mind," Steph said.

"It's not my business what happened between you all."

Vance shook his head in disgust. "You were happy to pitch in with your knife though, huh? An easy sidestep from tracking to killing us?"

Evan didn't look at Vance. "Gotta represent, but I was going to let him do the killing part. He figured you'd go for the Jeep so he got there first and drained the gas. He's enjoying this whole thing a lot more than I am."

Steph waited until Vance had zip-tied Evan's ankles before she stowed her weapon, filled with gratitude that she hadn't had to use it. She felt shaky and drained. They'd actually done it. Thanks to Chloe, they'd captured one of their two enemies.

Vance checked Evan's pockets for weapons. "Only the knife." He tucked the folded blade into his own pocket. "And this." He removed a radio and waved it at her.

She picked the cell up from where Evan had dropped it. "And this."

Vance grinned. "Now we're talking."

"Not gonna help you. Cell's pretty much

useless up here," Evan said. "Should have brought a satellite phone like Ferris has. My calls don't go through and my texts are hit-or-miss too."

"Don't kid a kidder, Evan. Your satellite radio works fine and you've got a GPS tracker on it, right? So the big boss knows where you are?"

Evan scowled.

"Code to unlock your phone?" Vance asked. "I'd like to see what you and Ferris have been chatting about. That'll make some nice evidence for the cops."

Evan scowled. "You're such a hotshot, figure it out yourself."

Vance yanked Evan's hand out and jammed his thumb on the button. "This way will work." The screen glowed and he frowned. "You've been efficient about deleting your texts and voice mails. Afraid you'll get in trouble?"

He scowled. "Not gettin' paid enough to stick my neck out too much."

Vance and Steph exchanged a look.

Vance's fingers danced over the tiny device and he frowned. "He's telling the truth. No texting, no calling."

"He's supposed to radio me for a report any minute now."

Vance grinned. "Don't worry. We'll make sure he gets one."

Evan stared in surly silence.

Steph cocked her chin. "Why would you throw your life away on Ferris? You don't trust him, clearly. Maybe you're afraid he's going to get rid of you when this is all over since you're a witness to his plans?"

Evan's mouth worked as he stared at his boots. "I only wanted the money. I didn't know it involved murder. Got in over my head until it was too late to bail."

Vance whistled. "Man, I'd be scared too if I were you, Ev, to be working for Ferris. Cops think he had a family of four murdered for crossing him. Did you know that? And he killed Elizabeth, the contest coordinator, and Steph's volunteer partner,

Gina. Six people dead already because of him. You'd make an easy seventh."

Sweat popped out on Evan's forehead. "I want to get out of here. Forget the whole thing. Untie me and you'll never hear from me again."

Vance smirked. "Uh-huh, I totally believe that. No way you'd tell Ferris our whereabouts in order to get your payout, right? 'Cuz you're such an upstanding, trustworthy guy?"

Steph knew that's exactly what Evan would do if they let him go. He'd put a lot of sweat and skin into the game and he'd want his pay. Plus, he was probably worried what Ferris would do to him if he took off with the job unfinished. Ferris knew where he lived, after all. Six people murdered. Vance was right. Ferris wouldn't bat an eyelash about killing Evan too.

"Where's the horse?" Vance asked. "We might have to borrow him."

"Nope. He's loose. He's used to being on his own and he's sure not going to let anyone on him but me if you do manage to catch him, which you won't."

"Fine. I'm no cowboy anyway." Vance examined the radio. "We'll be sure to send someone to collect you and your horse when the police get here."

Evan's eyes widened. "Don't you get it? Ferris is waiting for the opportune moment. He's got plenty of ammo and help. You'll be dead by the time any cops arrive."

Vance ignored him, continuing to flip through the phone. He looked over his shoulder at Steph. The gleam in his eyes intensified as a plan seemed to form. It was almost like she could see him assembling the pieces in his brain as she did the same.

"Tired of running?" she said softly.

"Beyond tired."

They smiled at each other in understanding. The only way to stop Ferris was to take control. Vance stowed Evan's phone along with the radio. "Rope?" he asked.

She tossed him a coil of white nylon. Vance used the rope to tie him to the tree. He was seated, his back to the trunk, fairly sheltered from the rain.

Evan didn't struggle, simply gaped. "You're not really going to leave me here, are you?"

"Yep," Vance said cheerfully. "Thought I was joking, huh?"

His eyebrows zinged up. "But what if you both get killed and no one finds me in time? I could starve to death or get eaten by mountain lions."

Vance considered. "Don't think they'd like the taste of you, but I guess you'd better hope Ferris doesn't win. If we don't get out of this alive, chances are you won't either."

"But..." Evan clamped his mouth closed and snorted. "So much for easy money."

Vance smiled. The smile and the sweat and the stubble somehow only served to make him more handsome.

"No such thing as easy money, didn't

you ever learn that?" Vance dropped two protein bars, a pack of pretzels and two bottles of water within reach. "Make it last, Ev. We'll double back to get you when we can or send help the moment we take Ferris's sat phone from him."

Evan groaned. "That'll never happen."

"Glass-half-empty kinda guy, huh?" Vance tossed an emergency blanket over Evan's lap. He would be able to unfold it, even with tied wrists. If he was extremely resourceful, he could find a sharp rock and saw his way loose, maybe locate his wayward horse, but that would take a while and he'd have no phone or access to a radio.

"He's going to yell," Steph said as Vance stood back.

"I'd be disappointed if he didn't. With the storm, I don't think anyone will hear him, and besides—" he grinned and wiggled Evan's radio "—Ferris is gonna think good old Ev here is somewhere entirely different."

The knowledge that Ferris would be privy to their exact location made her shiver.

Vance gave Evan a salute. "Hang in there, Ev. Catch you on the flip side."

Evan's cheeks went red.

"Ready to put the next part of our scheme into action?" Vance said. She could tell he was still flush from their victory.

"I need to do one thing first." She went to Chloe and gave her the signal. Chloe bounded up and galloped over to Evan, skidding to a stop practically on his lap.

"Call it off," Evan shouted.

"It's a she and you won't be bitten. She just wants her prize."

Ears flapping and glee in every line of her body, Chloe sniffed him all over, sprinkling him with slobber. Then she circled once and sat. Victory. Steph kneeled, rubbed the dog thoroughly and gave her a handful of jerky treats. She tossed one to Pudge too. He'd been a stalwart companion. "You're a good dog, Chloe. That was a champion find."

Her elation dimmed. Now would begin the second phase and it would be an excruciating effort to bring their real enemy to his knees.

She brought out the maps and she and Vance pored over them.

Their survival depended on making the right choice.

ELEVEN

Vance mulled it all over as they trekked over a series of steep climbs and bone-jarring descents. It would be a long hike to the spot where they'd chosen to enact their plan. Every rise brought yet another massive slice of untouched terrain into view. The wilderness felt endless, as if they were on some far-flung planet inhabited by only two exhausted humans and their hardworking canines. *And a killer. Don't forget that.* His shins screamed from the uneven trail and Pudge was a dead weight in his arms. Fortunately, Chloe was maintaining a good clip, but Steph was struggling, though she did her best to hide it.

The tracking contest was scheduled to end that night. The fact was both a plus

and a minus. With the competition con-
cluded, and Stephanie still not returned
after supposedly waiting out the weather
in a hotel as Ferris's fake message indicated, her family would be in rescue mode.
Unfortunately, he'd not left a hard return
date with Lettie, or she might have alerted
the authorities herself earlier. Nothing to
be accomplished by dwelling on that. Ferris, no doubt, would feel the hours dwin-
dling too, as dedicated to his mission as
they were to theirs. The man was determined to make sure they never set foot
back into civilization, the same punishment his father had received. What a family.

"Hey," Steph said, poking at his arm.

"What?"

"You're thinking and you walk too fast
when you're thinking. Besides, I want to
be in on the planning." She shoved the
bangs from her forehead. "No more bash-
ing drones and surprising me."

He laughed and lowered Pudge to the

ground, holding in the groan that wanted to escape. His failure weighed him down more than his overweight pal. He could avoid the issue, but it didn't feel right to cover up, not with her, not anymore. "I've been thinking about how we came to be in this predicament. Doesn't feel good to know Ferris led me here like a barnyard sheep, left the pamphlet for the competition for me to find. I did exactly what he intended, and I didn't suspect a thing. Some bounty hunter, huh?"

"I didn't suspect anything either. We were both bamboozled."

He quirked a smile. "Somehow that word makes it sound like less of a failure, but I was tracking the guy, Steph. It was my job to find him and I didn't and now we're here." *You're here, Steph. Because of me.* He could take the punishment he deserved for his stupidity, but he couldn't stomach her paying for his errors. And he didn't even want to think about Aunt Lettie finding out that the family who'd ultimately pushed her son into suicide was roaming free and spreading more terror around the world.

He was surprised when she slid her hand into his. "This isn't all on you. You tried to warn me. I didn't listen. We both got ourselves into this mess."

He laced his fingers through hers, the connection buoying his confidence. "And we're going to get out of it. Together."

"Still optimistic we can capture Ferris?"

"Absolutely. The timeline is shrinking for him to make a move. He's only got today before people start realizing you're missing."

"I thought of that too. Also, any minute now, he's going to check in with Evan via the radio when the guy doesn't report as scheduled. Ferris will either track him down, figuring it's a communication glitch, or Evan's had an accident or…"

"Either way he's going to need to follow Evan's GPS tracker and come see for himself, which is why our plan is a good one."

"He won't be an easy takedown like Evan was," she said.

"We chose the location carefully. This campground you spotted midway up the trail. It's flat with one main access. There are bound to be places we can get a bead on him. Spot him coming." And at minimum that campground would mean shelter. A secondary consideration, but his limbs were wooden with cold and the dogs were only protected so much by their raincoats from the steady drizzle. Unfortunately, it would be a full day's hike to get to the campground. Steph was trying hard to keep the pace, but she could not disguise her limp.

Her foot landed wrong and she cried out. His sudden grab was the only thing that kept her on her feet.

"You okay?"

"Sure, but maybe a quick rest?"

"Right." The dogs sniffed the rain-washed rocks and Steph selected the flattest, driest one she could find and settled onto it. Her eyes were smudged underneath with dark circles of fatigue and her mouth was tight with pain. She hauled up the right leg of her pants. He wasn't surprised to find her sock was tinged with blood that seeped up from her heel.

He wanted to chide her for not speaking up earlier about the severity of the wound, but that wouldn't help the situation. "Why don't I administer a little first aid, since we're stopped and all?"

"I can get by. Nothing major." She fumbled with the knotted laces until he pushed her hands out of the way.

"Good, because I'm only skilled in minor stuff."

She acquiesced, no doubt her pain winning out over her pride.

He worked the double knots loose and eased her foot from the boot. The heel of the sock was adhered to the skin with dried blood. From the water bottle he poured a splash of liquid onto the material until it came loose. "Looks rough. I can see why it's causing you pain."

She shrugged. "Normally I alternate pairs of boots and change socks frequently, but this hasn't been exactly a routine expedition."

"True that." He opened the first-aid kit. "This is going to sting, Wolfe. Sorry." The antiseptic washed away the grit and fibers. She stiffened but didn't make a sound. Chloe somehow intuited her pain anyway and came over to snuffle her chin. Pudge followed suit until she had two damp cheeks and a lap full of interested canines.

"Thanks, guys," she said, wiping the doggy saliva away.

Vance dabbed an ointment onto her ravaged skin and applied a bandage. He pulled dry socks from her pack. He was going to slide them on so quickly she wouldn't have time to protest his help, but she edged her feet away.

"I can do it."

He reached out and took her hands in his,

the soft ball of socks nestled between them. She was cold, so cold, and he wished his touch would lend her warmth. He caught her amber gaze for a moment, the color of rich honey. "There is nothing more important to me right now than helping you."

She suddenly looked away and he knew he shouldn't have said it, not with such earnestness, but his defenses were falling away with each mile and it was the honest truth. He would give anything to spare her from more pain. *Lighten the mood, Silverton.* "And I'm tired, but if I have to chase you around this forest and jam these socks on your pretty feet, I will."

"I..." She twisted to look at him. "You think my feet are pretty?"

She'd latched on to that? Mystifying. "Yes, ma'am. You got yourself two dainty princess feet right there."

"I always thought the toes were too long, nothing like my sister Kara's."

He regarded her toes solemnly. "I confess I've never seen your sister's toes, but these piggies are beauts."

She actually giggled and her momentary relaxation allowed him the chance to roll the socks onto her feet.

Her eyes closed for a moment and an expression of contentment spread across her features. "Can't believe a pair of dry socks could feel so amazing."

Amazing. He'd given her that with a pair of socks. He could have danced. "And for my final performance," he said, unfurling two plastic bags he'd taken from her supply and sliding them over the socks. "No way we can get your boots dry right now, but this should provide something of a barrier." He eased on her boots and rolled the extra plastic down so it was hardly visible.

When he was done, he offered his palm with a flourish and helped her to stand. "Better?"

"Loads," she said. "Thank you."

He wondered why he felt so incredible about being able to help her into dry socks and plastic bags. It was more rewarding than any bust he'd ever made, any race he'd ever won. Flushed with happiness, he gave the dogs two treats each before they hit the trail.

They journeyed on as the day slipped into late afternoon and cold shadows mingled with the rain. He tried Evan's phone again and she tried hers. No reception. No call from Ferris on the radio.

An hour passed into two and when he'd almost decided they'd made a wrong turn, Steph grabbed his arm.

"There."

The trail ahead flattened out into a wide sweep of level ground with a dozen canvas tents erected atop wooden frames. Everything seemed in good condition, buttoned up well for the winter. A river rushed behind the campground and the mountain peaks soared above, lost in the velvet puffs of clouds. It would be the ideal place for a wilderness adventure. Not that he ever planned on adventuring in the wilderness again. Only destinations with well-paved roads and good cell coverage would be his aim and nowhere too far-flung from hot coffee and washers and dryers.

He pointed. "That's got to be the office cabin to the left. Guest tents and two bathhouses. The squat building in the center is probably a dining hall or something along those lines. We'll get inside a tent, activate a lantern to draw attention. Hopefully, Ferris will think it's Evan."

Steph nodded. "The dogs and I will find another tent cabin to hole up in, where we can get a visual. I wonder how much time we'll have."

The tent they chose for the lantern decoy was musty but dry. He hauled a small table close to the window and set the lantern on it. The glow would certainly be visible to Ferris. They both flinched as the radio crackled in Vance's pocket. Stomach tight, he drew it out.

Ferris's voice was muted and tinny. "Answer me, Evan. Why are you near the campground? Why haven't you communicated with me?"

Vance put his shirt over the speaker. "Drone broke," he said. "Tracked 'em here. They're approaching." He turned the radio squawk button. "Trouble hearing you."

"What do you mean the drone broke?" Ferris demanded.

Vance played once more with the buttons, as if his conversation was being interrupted by static. "Can't…hear you."

"Just hold in place and keep them in your sights, you oaf," Ferris snarled. "I'm coming to you. Don't do anything until I get there. It'll be three hours, minimum, if I don't blow a tire on the way."

The radio cut out. Vance returned it to his pocket.

"I guess we have our timeline," he said slowly.

"I guess we do." She blew out a breath, which steamed the air. "Better go see what our accommodations look like."

The canvas tents were secured only by

strong zippers. The interior of the second platform tent was stripped bare, and the raised cots sat on wooden frames with no bedding. Aged floors showed slight warping and possible rodent visitations if the dogs' sniffing was any indication. They put down their gear and walked back to the nearest bathhouse.

The door was secured by a sturdy padlock. He turned around to find Steph holding two rocks out for him. "Your padlock trick, right?"

He grinned. "Look at you, my lock-picking apprentice. I'm sure we can explain a busted lock to the park service, considering." He got in on the first whack. Inside, the bathhouse smelled of cleanser and mildew. There were two stalls with plastic shower curtains and a separate toilet area.

To her delight, Steph found the sink faucets working. Instantly, the two dogs reared up on their hind legs and shoved their muzzles into the flowing water, lapping noisily. The humans laughed, enjoying their companions' excitement.

While she dried the dogs with a paper towel, he strode to what appeared to be a closet and opened it. A fairly new hot-water heater beckoned. *If this works, it'll be a game changer.* With a match from his pocket, he lit the pilot light and continued to explore the closet, where he found a stack of towels.

"Steph?" he said.

She was washing her hands in the sink. "Yes?"

"Could I interest you in a hot shower and a clean towel?"

She whirled. "Don't even tease about that, Silverton."

"No teasing, ma'am. This is an eighty-gallon water heater, which should take about an hour to heat, by my calculation."

"How do you…?" She broke off, eyes wide. "Forget I asked. Marines do things and they know stuff. If you're right about this one, I'll bake you a cake."

He folded his arms. "What kind?"

"Any kind," she said breathlessly.

He stroked his chin, pretending to think it over. "I have specifications. Not any old variety will do. I require carrot cake with cream-cheese frosting."

"Okay."

"And the cake part should have raisins and bits of pineapple mixed in there. Not pineapple chunks, mind you—tidbits. That's what Aunt Lettie calls them."

Her mouth quirked. "All right."

"With flecks of nuts. Walnuts, not pecans. And the frosting needs to be thick on the outside and in the middle part too, where the layers stick together."

"You require layers?"

"Yes, minimum two, and back on the frosting topic, it should have those blobby swirls on top."

"Blobby swirls? You mean rosettes?"

He snapped his fingers. "That's it. Rosettes. I need rosettes on my cake."

She stopped him with a raised hand.

"You're really milking this for everything you can get."

"Hot shower," he said in a singsong voice. "What's a measly cake compared to the joy that will bring?"

She laughed, a light silvery sound he hadn't heard since they'd dated. "All right. Carrot cake with two layers, raisins, tidbits and rosettes."

"And nut flecks. Don't forget those."

"And nut flecks. I can make that happen. Kara won't mind helping me out if I need a consultation."

"Excellent. While we let the water heat, how about we choose a tent for dining and resting activities?"

"Fine, but..." A frown stole the joy from her expression. "Should we be thinking about showers and cakes and resting while we wait for a murderer to arrive to kill us?"

"We have a good three hours, remember? And he's not going to kill us. We're going to neutralize him before he can make a move." He held the door open for her and the dogs. "And what's more he's not getting any cake in prison. Ever."

They decided on a tent cabin positioned so they'd have a clear view of the one below, where they'd placed the lantern, and the road beyond. Inside, Steph's teeth chattered and his hands were icy in spite of the thick canvas that kept off the wind and rain. What he'd give to make a roaring campfire outside. He'd bundle her close, and they and the dogs would watch the flames dance and the stars emerge on the heels of the storm. *Don't let your mind drift right now, buddy.* He blinked and the daydream popped and vanished. Cold tent, hungry belly, feet blistered and bloody and Ferris on the way. Those were the realities to keep front and center.

But other feelings filtered in anyway. Gratitude, for one. They were alive and Steph would get her shower and God would help them survive, like He'd been doing for the past four days. *Thanks, God. Sorry for the grumbling.*

Steph fed the dogs and offered more water, while he used the burner to heat Steph's dehydrated whole wheat mac and cheese for the humans. The abnormally orange kind out of the blue box was undoubtedly way better but he'd have the good manners not to say so. Only four packets left from her supply. He didn't have much more, just some pouches of nuts and the remnants of the candy. He could probably inhale the whole lot in one sitting and still not be full.

The salty pasta soothed his raw throat. He and Steph devoured every morsel and scraped all traces from the foil packets. He craved more but at least it momentarily quieted the major stomach rumbling. After they finished, he handed her the baggie with the remaining half dozen M&M's. "Almost done with this adventure. Might as well polish them off."

With a grin, she took the bag and began to divide them up.

"No need. All six for you, Steph." He patted his stomach. "Watching the carbs."

Her giggles turned to guffaws and he joined in. Their laughter intertwined, drifted, circled through the musty old tent. Was there ever such a joyful sound? There shouldn't be any laughter here, not now, yet somehow God made room for it.

She doled out two candies, savoring one at a time and stowing the other four. "These will be the celebration candies for the moment we capture Ferris."

"Hear! Hear!" he said. "Be another half hour before your hot water's ready. Might as well take a snooze." She nodded. He unrolled one of the sleeping bags on the raised platform bed and she lay down on it. Before he could even cover her with the other, she was asleep.

He brushed the hair from her face and snuggled the fabric around her.

He settled down on the empty bunk

across from her, elbows resting on his aching knees. The risk of what they were attempting circled in his gut. So much piled up against them. Maybe they should have separated, like he'd suggested. She might have had a chance to escape. But she'd wanted them to face Ferris together. Somewhere deep down she'd decided to trust him again. The very thing he'd longed for, coveted, and now he'd gotten it and he was scared he'd let her down again. Only this time, she'd pay with her life and Chloe's.

"Lord, I've messed up so many things," he murmured quietly. "And I don't deserve any special treatment, but please let me get this woman and these dogs out of here safely. Show me how to do it and give me the strength and Your protection."

When he was done, he tried to fight the fatigue and achiness by cleaning and loading his weapon, reorganizing his pack, running the plan in an endless loop in his mind. He wasn't going to sleep, in case Ferris arrived before the estimated three hours. The dogs had no such problem, lying side by side, Pudge snoring.

The time elapsed and he touched her shoulder. "Ready for your hot shower, sleepyhead?"

She blinked, then leaped to her feet. "I'll race you."

"Not with your heel all bandaged up. A brisk walk will do."

The dogs roused themselves and trotted after their humans. Pudge applied his nose to the ground in similar fashion to Chloe. Maybe the dog was actually learning some tracking skills. Vance puffed with pride. "I knew Pudgy had hidden talents."

Steph considered. "He's done really great." She reached for his hand and squeezed. "And so have you. And I'm not just saying that because you're supplying a hot shower."

He tucked her arm in his, intending to savor their closeness until the moment she left him again. "Flattery will get you everywhere," he joked. Her arm remained linked with his until they reached the bathhouse.

"Your shower awaits, madam," he said, holding the door open for her.

"Why thank you, kind sir." She went in and he heard the sound of the shower running while he stood outside. Her ecstatic squeal of glee confirmed that the water heater was functioning properly. He wished he'd recorded that sound of her happiness.

"Am I a stud or what?" he crowed. Pudge swiped a rubbery tongue over Vance's shin to confirm he thought so too.

Still grinning, Vance watched the dogs meander through the puffs of steam that emanated from under the door. He peered up, the rain having subsided into a mist. The clouds were down to ragged wisps that revealed swaths of inky sky.

Somewhere above was a patchwork of constellations, scads of stars shining steadily, though he could only see a sprinkling of them. A memory ripped at his se-

renity. He recalled standing in the front
yard of his mother's home at some ridiculous hour with the stars twinkling overhead. He'd been trying to find the car keys
his mother had tossed from the house in
a rage since she was up throughout the
night as the disease advanced. Even with
alarms engaged to let him know if she
snuck out, she'd flung open the door and
shouted insults at him as she'd lobbed the
key ring into the grass, which he'd not had
time to cut.

He'd hit bottom at that moment, crawling
on hands and knees in his frantic search
with the wet grass soaking the knees of
his jeans. Her shrieks flew at him like
sharp arrows, insults piercing him from a
woman who'd loved him all his life. Why?
He'd cried out to God then, for help, for
strength, for comfort that didn't come
from a bottle.

And their neighbor, dear Lettie, had
driven up without warning that very morning, to soothe his mother, tuck her back

into bed with prayers and song and help him find the keys. Lettie was the help God had sent, and he'd not been able to repay her, except to promise he'd spend his life putting Ferris back behind bars. Ferris, the man who'd turned her son into an informer, the person responsible for assassinating a family, waiting for his chance to add to his list of kills.

Steph's high soprano trickled out to him and he felt such a rush of pleasure and a deep sense of blessing that he'd been able to comfort her. Had Lettie felt similar? Was she blessed by being able to bless him and his mother? Did it assuage her own pain to lessen someone else's agony?

It was a thought he hadn't entertained before. Such a refreshing idea. He'd talk about it with Lettie when he got back, right after he told her he'd put away the criminal that her son, Jack, had let himself fall in with. The next few hours...

His mother's words as he'd driven her to the memory care home rang in his ears.

You hate me. You're sending me away.

He prayed Steph and Lettie were right and he'd shown his love with actions even when his mother thought he'd betrayed her by moving her to a memory care facility, where she'd passed away. *I hope you know I only wanted the best for you, Mama. I miss you.* The grief rose outward until it engulfed him. So much pain. So many regrets.

He stopped, pulled in a breath as deep as his lungs would hold and exhaled slowly, forcing his thoughts to the here and now. The humans and dogs were alive, and Steph was relishing a hot shower. He was sober and cherished by Lettie, a woman who had no reason to step into his life except that God had prompted her to. And he and Steph were reconnecting, at least at some level.

So much love. So many memories. The good and the bad. He prayed once again they'd all live to experience more of the tumultuous journey God planned for them. He shoved his hands in his pockets and breathed deeply of the mountain air until Steph emerged bundled in her clothes again and with an expression of utter bliss. "That was the best shower of my entire life."

He chuckled. "Well worth the effort it's going to take to bake the cake?"

"Absolutely."

He reached out and touched her shoulder. "I'm glad." She turned her head to look at him and he moved her closer, feeling the warmth of her body from the hot shower.

"You okay?" she asked. "You look… pensive."

"Yeah. I was…" Nothing had been promised. The end could be nearer than either of them imagined. He felt the words welling up and decided to let them out before he thought better of it. "I was thinking. After we get clear of this, I'd like to invite you over for dinner, wherever Pudge and I find to live, I mean."

Her churning thoughts were almost palpable. Had he erred? He hurried on.

"I've learned how to cook chili after much trial and error and I have some boxes of Girl Scout cookies left. I'll buy us some cornbread to go with it. What do you say?" he asked, then rushed on. "We could, maybe, start again."

Her soft exhale was a white puff in the night. "Not sure that's a good idea."

He felt a pinprick to his soul but he soldiered on. "Why not?"

"We're different people, Vance. Completely. I had a lot of time to think about it since we broke up. I'm serious and intense. You're relaxed and fun-loving. I plan and you're a seat-of-the-pants kinda person. It's just…" Her words dropped off for a moment and she tapped him lightly on the chest. "We had our shot. Probably wouldn't have worked out anyway, right? Even if we hadn't broken up over the job."

Right? Absolutely wrong, but if she didn't want him, then it was the end of the line. The warm optimism he'd felt a moment before was smothered by the pain that bloomed in his heart.

"You're a good man, Vance Silverton. I hope we'll be friends forever."

Friends was not what he wanted and he wasn't quite ready to give up. "Opposites can be a good thing," he said stubbornly. "Would you want to date another version of yourself? Relationships are supposed to make the other person better."

She remained silent, not quite looking at him.

He was losing her; maybe he'd already lost her. The despair widened, and he stepped back and cleared his throat. "Anyway it was just a dinner invite."

"Sure. And it's very sweet, but…we should focus on bigger picture things now. A few more hours and this will all be over. Critical time, right?"

"Yes." But for some reason, the picture that kept flashing across his consciousness was one of him and her, together, safe and

back in love. But that required two willing participants and she'd made her position clear. *Dream on, Vance.*

So many good memories.

So much regret.

He'd have to learn to live with both.

TWELVE

Steph was practically delirious at being warm and clean, but even those sensations could not quite strip away the lingering doubt about what she'd said to Vance. He'd made it clear—he wanted to start over. She'd been given another chance to pick up the relationship that ended in pain for both of them. And she'd turned him away.

It was true, every word she'd said. They were complete opposites, wired differently, through and through. Their recent affection was the outgrowth of a bizarre, stressful situation over which they could exercise no control. That affection butted right up against the tough, invisible wall she'd built around her emotions when it came to Vance. Ironic that it was in a place with no walls whatsoever that she'd realized the overwhelming dimensions of the one she'd constructed.

As much as she felt Vance tugging at her heart, she was not ready to let him breach that barrier. Or more accurately perhaps, she wasn't willing to provide the ladder. Over that, she still had control and she'd cling to it regardless of their current situation.

But something's changed, her spirit whispered. *Vance isn't the person you knew. And you aren't the same, Steph.* Emotions new and fresh and startling were racing around her body in spite of the fact that it was absolutely the worst timing ever.

Determined to leave the thoughts behind, she followed Vance to the empty tent, where the dogs promptly fell into another snooze. She admired their ability to live in the moment. There was still no cell signal and her texts were lost in a swirl of dots that never seemed to send. "One text. Why can't I send one lousy text?"

Vance wasn't listening but was busily peering through the binoculars out the plastic-covered window. "Nothing so far."

She crept up next to him and peered through her own binoculars.

"Stay down, Steph," he said automatically, glasses swiveling to take in the campground and the wooded trail below.

She bristled, her unsettled feelings rushing to the surface. "I'm part of this team too."

"Right. I'm only saying we don't need two directors for this show. I'll take care of recon. You back me up after I corner him."

Here was confirmation of why she was right about them. Even now, after everything they'd endured, he'd dismissed her. She folded her arms and glared at him.

He finally looked away from his lenses and realized. He sank down on the plank floor to face her. "What did I say? Something dumb, judging by your expression."

She shook her head. "Never mind."

"Nope." He put down the glasses and folded his hands in his lap. "We've got a while before he'll be here. You made it clear I won't see much of you after we return to civilization." The hurt flashed in his eyes. "What?"

She unclenched her jaw. "You got all bossy."

"Oh, is that it? Sorry." He flashed a lazy smile. "Occupational hazard."

Of course. And totally acceptable, for most of the force. The old anger rekindled and left her grasping for words. She finally landed on a reply. "Easy for a man to say that, Vance."

He cocked his chin. "What do you mean?"

Her frustration was too close to the surface but she forced an exhale. "It's not important right now, considering."

His jaw tensed. "Steph, we're not going to talk once we shake this off, except for the cake delivery, and we're about to have a knock-down-drag-out with a killer.

Might get a little messy so I think there's no better moment to clear the air. Spill it."

She shoved back the bangs from her forehead. "You have no idea how hard it is to be a woman cop, do you?"

His forehead crinkled in confusion. "I can imagine some of it, a woman in what's still a male-dominated profession, but clearly I don't have a complete picture. Tell me."

A flush of heat crept up her neck and she suddenly felt ridiculous. Why was she talking about this? Now? To a man she'd just condemned to the friend zone? With Ferris closing in to trying and kill them? But the words came out anyway, as if the water had started to pour through the tiny hole in the dam, taking all the bracing with it. "As a man, you react and you don't have to overthink how you're coming across to others. A woman in a leadership role on the other hand…can't be too girly, or they'll see you as weak. Too pushy and they'll accuse you of being a harpy. Anything a male cop has to put up with is twice as hard for a woman, and you know what?" Unexpected tears welled and she blinked them away, forcing her chin up. "I was a good cop, a very good cop, in spite of all that."

"No argument there."

And she was right back in the hurt again of what had happened between them. "I was looking outside the department because I knew there were five guys ahead of me for promotion including you, three of whom were long-timers, which meant I wouldn't have a shot at detective for years, maybe ever."

He started to rebut but she cut him off.

"Whisper Valley never had a female in the detective role. Ever. There were only two women in the whole department when I left and for the past ten years all lateral transfers from other departments were male, even though dozens of seasoned women cops applied right along with those men."

"Steph, I…" He sighed. "I never thought about it that way." He slumped. "As soon as I let it slip that you were looking elsewhere, I destroyed your chance at that promotion. It didn't occur to me that it might be your only chance for a while. Never really considered that your opportunities would be fewer and farther between than mine." He waited for her to say more.

"Most male cops in Whisper Valley don't really get it."

"But I should have. I'm sorry."

She didn't want to go into the other part. He'd already apologized, hadn't he? But it came tumbling out as she stared at the warped floorboards. "What hurt most wasn't the lost opportunity, even though that was painful, but the fact that I didn't matter to you as much as the promotion did."

He grimaced. "You did, Steph. You mattered, but my pride and my plans got in the way for a minute."

"It wasn't a momentary failure, Vance.

We were both applying for that job and we knew someone had to lose. I was prepared for that. But you took something I'd shared with you, my trust in you, and tossed it away. I didn't think you were that kind of person. It's hard enough to love someone..." She snapped her mouth shut. Too late. He'd heard the *L* word. Completely mortifying.

She hadn't realized until that very moment why Vance's actions had hurt so much. Because in order to be the best at what she did in a male-dominated arena, she'd striven to control every detail of her life. Loving someone, loving Vance, was the most out-of-control thing she could ever consider, and she'd done it anyway. Hook, line, sinker.

Thrown away her control.

Because of him.

He touched her hand. "Steph, I'm sorry. I hurt you. I've never been sorrier for anything in my life. And what's more, I didn't know all those things about how hard it was for you on the force. I should have. A man has to understand the realities of the woman in his life. We'd dated long enough that I should have known. And all cops should know and understand. We have enough enemies outside the force. We're brothers and sisters in blue. One family."

She was still fighting back the persistent tears. There was a possibility they were going to die, so why should it matter that they cleared the air anyway? Here she was talking about things in the past that could not be changed. She couldn't possibly control the tiniest thing about their present situation either. Instead of measuring out the words, fashioning her next comment, she let her thoughts gush out. "I know you're sorry. You said so before and I believe you were sincere. I truly do, and I'm sorry for not making things clear to you earlier and bringing this all up now. I guess… I wasn't finished being mad about it."

He extended his palm to her with the most tender look she'd ever witnessed on a man's face. "Will you forgive me, Steph? Not just about the job thing, but for breaking your heart? Your trust? All of it?"

A lump formed in her throat as she struggled to answer. Yes? No? A little of both? What was the real answer?

His eyes sought hers.

She could brush him off and turn away.

But maybe this was her only chance. God had given her a moment, one slender tick of the clock, to let Him work in her, show her how to forgive, revive her heart, which had turned to stone. Forgiveness was the only way to heal both of them. Even if her love of Vance didn't return to what it had been, this was the way forward.

She reached out and twined her fingers with his. Her silent response was enough.

His expression lit from within, as if the sun had risen inside and spilled across his face. She felt the warmth of it deep in her own soul. He bent to kiss her fingers and she felt his tears. Her anger was good and truly gone now, the soul spot it had occupied filled with something warm and soft and healing. No matter what happened, she would remember with gratitude that God had set both of them free in that wild nowhere.

Pudge intruded on the moment by jerking his head up and flopping one ear as he listened intently.

"Caught a sound, boy?"

Chloe alerted a second later too, scurrying over to Pudge.

Vance again lifted his binoculars, only now he gestured for her to join him. She squeezed close and they both scanned the terrain.

Two soft golden flickers drew their attention from deep in the woods. Headlights, definitely.

"It's him," Vance said. "He's got your car. Saved those spark-plug wires. Wonder why he's not driving whatever he rode in on."

Steph's heart slammed into her ribs.

Fifteen minutes more. Maybe less? The lights flickered in and out of view along the twisted trail through the woods.

"I'm going to make my way to the pinch point, where he'll enter the campground," Vance said. "I'd love to blow out the tires, but we'll need a vehicle to get out of here. I will if I have to though. Agreed?"

She nodded. Whatever it took, they had to stop him now, gain control. "I'll be in position at your three beside the bathhouse, lay down some cover fire or take him out if I get the chance."

He grimaced. "It really pains me to know you're a much better shot than I am."

"Deal with it, Silverton."

They checked their flashlights, which would be their only means of communication if things went wrong. "Two flashes if he gets away from you since I won't have a clear line of sight from your side."

"He won't. He'll have to stop and go on foot when he hits the edge of the parking area to access the campground. Soon as he opens that driver's-side door, he's my prisoner."

My prisoner. Her skin grew cold. What if the plan went awry? Ferris already had superior firepower and plenty of ammo, a car, communication. What if Evan had gotten loose somehow? But there was no way they could have reconnected, since Ferris was tracking Evan's radio right to the campground.

Doubt still nagged at her. What if they'd overlooked something? Vance stopped her cartwheeling thoughts with a squeeze to her wrist.

"Steph, this is all going to be over soon."

The shimmer in his gaze went right through her but it didn't eclipse the fear that took hold deep in her bones. How tragic would it be if they finally reached a place of forgiveness, only to be slaughtered by Ferris Grinder?

"Just...no going after him with a branch or anything, right? If it goes sideways, we regroup and make a new plan."

"We'll see what the mood calls for," he said breezily. He pulled on his pack.

"Maybe I'll take you up on that offer," she blurted, fiddling with her own.

He jerked a look at her. "What offer?"

"Dinner, like you said. A bowl of chili when I deliver the cake. I could do some quick lessons with Pudge. You need someone to help you because he is desperately lacking in training."

Pudge looked up at his name, tongue lolling.

Vance beamed. "That'd be great, absolutely fantastic. Chili it is. But I'll have to take up the training thing later with Pudge. He's going to need a long vacation after this. I mean he went from cowering in fear of his roommate in the shelter to tracking an assassin. He probably needs a few spa treatments or something."

"Don't we all?"

He leaned down and kissed her then, lightly, as if he was afraid of jostling the fragile connection between them.

Tingles swept through her body. She cupped his cheek. "Don't get hurt, okay? Please."

He kissed her again, a little more firmly, a little longer connection.

Her stomach clenched. "If he smells our trap I'll assist in taking out the tires."

"I won't need it."

She laughed. "Yes, you will."

With one final grin, he snuck off.

With her kiss warm on his lips, he crept out into the night. His limitations were frustrating. No means to communicate with Steph save a flashlight signal. This was truly a desperate, old-school scenario. He was confident anyway, encouraged by the thought of ending the torture. Ferris was already here and all they had to do was get him out of his car. Between him and Steph, they'd handle the rest. Ferris wasn't interested in dying, only killing, and he'd surrender when he realized he was out of options.

Besides, Steph was willing to eat his chili and help his dog.

If that wasn't a green light to rebuild their relationship, he didn't know what was. *Later, Romeo. Focus.* He silently counted the passing minutes.

Steph didn't signal that she was in place to the side of the bathhouse, the dogs shut safely in the cabin tent, for fear of tipping off Ferris, but she'd had time to settle into position. The lightness in his soul was euphoric. She'd forgiven him, she'd made him understand her deepest, truest feelings, and she was going to share a meal with him.

He restrained himself from whistling as he found the perfect shrubby nook to conceal himself. Ferris was closer now, winding his way along the twisty entrance road in Steph's car. The arrogance of him to take hers when he had a vehicle in which he'd arrived. Probably stroked his ego to use Steph's. Insult to injury. Smarter for

Ferris to have parked somewhere along the trail and gone the rest of the distance on foot since he'd be impossible to track in the dark, but Ferris wasn't one to do things the hard way and he wasn't expecting the trap that was coming. No, he'd gotten Evan to ride all over on horseback with his drone and feed information. Ferris would roll on up in his cushy vehicle, an assassin with all the creature comforts.

Vance yearned with everything in him to finish things. No more miserable nights in the cold with dehydrated food for dinner and every square inch of them scraped, bruised and bashed. Stephanie and her pretty toes would be out of here, along with their long-suffering dogs.

The car rolled closer, taking a sharp turn that brought Ferris out of view behind the rocks for a moment. Vance tamped down his glee at the thought that Ferris would return to jail for the rest of his life. He couldn't wait to tell Lettie. Justice wouldn't bind her heart together again, but it might help her sleep at night knowing Ferris wouldn't hurt anyone else's child.

"Come to Papa, Ferris. Just a bit further." He pulled his weapon and laid it next to him before pointing the binoculars again. The headlights bobbed and bounced, a weak glow in the face of all that darkness. He plotted it out in his mind. Ferris would pull up in the parking area, see the lantern in the decoy tent, confirmation that Evan was indeed waiting for him. He'd arm himself and get out of the car.

And Vance would make his move. Hopefully Steph wouldn't have to be involved at all. No shooting. Nice and neat.

The car slowed as it approached the last turn. Vance's fingers tensed on his gun. "Come on."

The vehicle idled as if Ferris was considering.

"What are you waiting for?" Vance muttered. He almost dropped the binoculars as the car executed a hasty U-turn. *What?*

No, this couldn't be happening. What had spooked him? Didn't matter. They weren't going to lose Ferris now. He prayed Ferris wasn't looking in his rear-view mirror as he flicked his flashlight beam once. What he wouldn't have given for a working cell phone, but Steph would probably intuit what he intended. She'd have seen Ferris's abrupt retreat.

Vance holstered his weapon in his belt and picked his way over the uneven ground as fast as he could. A straight shot through the woods would put him on an intercept course with the road where it coiled around the mountain. He'd have to shoot the tires out or disable Ferris through the windshield. Both difficult in the dark, but he'd do it.

Why would Ferris wait until he was almost at the camp and then jet away? What had given their plan away? Vance stumbled on a tree root and fell to one knee, the jarring pain flashing hot through his leg as he hopped up again. There was no time to slow and no way to track where Ferris was without risking missing him. On he jogged, leaping over rocks and crashing against branches he'd not detected. The land sloped down and the wind direction changed, diverted away from the mass of mountain. His destination was dead ahead. He pulled his weapon and crept forward until he could see the road below.

Taillights shone three yards away. While he got into position to take a shot, he realized the car was idling. *Why?*

He eased to the edge and lined up on the rear tire.

The car burst into motion, the driver's foot hard on the pedal.

Vance fired a shot that glanced off the rear fender. He was going for shot two when he stopped.

Why would Ferris turn away from the campground?

Why had he appeared to idle there for a moment?

Almost as if the driver was waiting…

Vance's stomach contracted to a tight fist.

Ferris hadn't fallen into their trap... because he'd planned one of his own.

The campground... Stephanie.

Vance whipped around and sprinted hard.

Steph couldn't imagine why Ferris had suddenly departed but she knew Vance had pursued him and she wasn't going to leave him without backup. She stowed the binoculars in her pack and worked out a bare-bones plan as she hurried around the bathhouse. She'd hustle after Vance, get close enough to signal him—he'd be expecting her to follow anyway—and find a position to shoot out Ferris's tires. Vance was probably going to try the same thing, but she'd have a better chance at success. Between the two of them, Ferris wasn't getting away.

Thanks to the hairpin turns in the road, they'd have an opportunity to short cut their way to intercept by hustling through the woods.

She'd have to move fast though, because Vance wasn't going to wait around for her to catch up. He'd go blasting away. Suspicion poked at her. What had given them away? She'd just cleared the corner of the bathhouse when a leg swept out, caught her ankle. The ground rushed to meet her as she fell.

THIRTEEN

The breath whooshed out of her. A moment later Ferris put a knee in the small of her back and a gun to the side of her head.

No. It could not be.

His breath was hot on her cheek. "Hello, Stephanie. Not quite what you were expecting, right?"

She tried to process the ruse. Vance was chasing someone else in the car they'd thought Ferris had been in. Had he freed Evan? They must have connected somehow. She'd not thought it possible but the pain in her spine from Ferris's weight made it crystal clear they'd miscalculated. Ferris had tricked them again. A scream built inside, but she tried to control her rising panic. She clamped her mouth shut, grit digging into her chin as he pressed her to the ground.

He stripped the handgun from her waistband. "Hoping to shoot me down, neat and tidy? Kill me like you did to my father? How unsportsmanlike."

"I didn't kill your father."

"You put him in prison. Same thing." He ground the gun into her skull. "Helplessness is a bad feeling, right? You're trapped, awaiting your fate. That's how I felt in jail. My dad too."

The scent of pine was strong in her nostrils. "Killing me isn't going to change anything."

"Of course it will—for me anyway and for your kin. Family ties are strong, aren't they, Steph? Your people will mourn your death and that's justice in my book."

"Not mine."

"Don't be so pretentious. You'd do whatever for your family. Grinders and Wolfes agree on that point. That makes us the same, you and me."

"No, it doesn't. I wouldn't murder any-one for my family."

He increased the pressure on her temple until she thought her skull would splinter.

"You would, if the circumstances were right." He hauled her to her feet and marched her to the shadows under the tree near the bathhouse. He kept her in front of him, far enough that she could not flail and knock him over or deliver a sat-isfying head butt. If she broke away, she'd be dead in moments. In the distance she heard Chloe howl. Her heart ached. What would happen to the dogs if she and Vance died here? They would die too, likely, of starvation if they weren't discovered quick enough. Or maybe Ferris would kill them also.

Plan, Steph. What's the plan?

Ferris forced her under the dripping branches. "Vance thinks he's following me right now. Dope. Does he have Evan's radio or do you?"

When she didn't answer he spun her

around and shoved her against the tree trunk. She banged the back of her head. He yanked a radio from a clip on his belt. "Vance's voice is far too deep to do a good Evan impersonation, by the way, but it was a noble effort for a dumb ex-cop."

She could only stare at him, desperate to find a way out of the deadly scenario.

He wriggled the radio. "This is where it gets fun."

Her stomach dropped.

"Silverton," he said into the radio. "It's Ferris. I'm here with your girl. Got ahead of you again and you didn't suspect a thing. You tore off after the car assuming I was the driver. You know what they say about assumptions. No wonder you both washed out as cops. Getting tired of being played yet?"

Stephanie's throat was tight with terror as the radio crackled with a response.

"If you hurt her, you will die." Vance's tone was so hard, so fierce, she almost didn't recognize it. *Just run, Vance. Get away.* But she knew with a surge of grief and love that he wouldn't. He would do what Ferris asked in an attempt to save her. Fear at what was about to happen flashed along her nerves.

"Don't—" she began to call out to Vance, but Ferris slammed a palm over her mouth so hard she tasted blood. He stepped away a few paces but didn't lower his weapon.

"You'll come to me," Ferris said into the radio. "I want you to see her die before I kill you."

See her die. It was a nightmare.

Vance's breathing was audible over the radio. "Ferris—"

Ferris cut him off. "You'll walk into the campground up the front drive. That's what's going to happen. If you do as I say, she'll die easy, one quick kill shot. If you don't…it will be long and extremely painful, I can promise you." He paused, listening to the sound of Chloe's barking, now accompanied by Pudge. "And then

I'll find the dogs and kill them and I'll make it last so they suffer too. That's your choice. I kill the woman and both dogs in the most agonizing way possible, or you deliver yourself to me and they go easily. If you decide to bolt and save your own skin, you'll be a dead man walking from then on. I'll scour every square inch of this wilderness until I find you."

"Not going to happen," Vance snapped.

"Yes, it is," Ferris said. "It's a matter of how it's going to happen and that's up to you. Ten minutes. If you're not at the entrance in ten minutes, their suffering is on your head." He fired a shot. She screamed as it streaked past, three inches from her cheekbone, boring into the tree next to where she stood.

"Ferris," Vance shouted but he turned off the radio and produced a rope.

"Turn around, grab the tree and give it a hug, Officer Wolfe."

She kept her hands at her sides, but he glowered at her. "I can tie you with your cooperation, or I can shoot you first and accomplish the same thing in a messier fashion. Either way, I need you in one place."

Stiffly, she held her arms around the trunk and he tied her wrists together, pinioning her in place. She fought back the enraged howl that wanted to force its way from her mouth. Instead, she pressed her cheek to the abrasive bark and tried to think. He wouldn't win, couldn't, not after what they'd endured, after the evil he and his father had brought on the world.

Vance would be showing up in a matter of moments. She had to figure out some way to help him or distract Ferris. The bark was rough, hardened by centuries of weather. She could use it to saw the rope if he'd turn his attention away. Breath held, she silently willed him to stop staring at her.

Her wish was answered a moment later when Ferris turned away to scan the road with his binoculars. Then he switched his focus to the trees that crowded in on every side along the sweep of road where Vance would approach. The Kevlar vest was strapped tight around his body, but he kept near the bathhouse to shield himself in case Vance took a shot.

Which was exactly what she would do in Vance's shoes, but he wasn't going to shoot wildly in the dark, at a distance. He'd have to get close enough that he was confident his bullet wouldn't hit her too. He wouldn't risk it. She scraped the rope against the bark. The abrasion caught on the nylon, biting into it.

Hurry.

She kept at it.

Chloe and Pudge were barking in unison, the sound carrying in the night air.

When Ferris spared a look at her, she had to stop.

He chuckled. "Have to admit, it would have been much faster if I'd shot you both a couple of days ago, but not nearly as much fun. This is drama, and I'll enjoy remembering it for the rest of my life."

She smothered the rage, the tears, the pain and fear. He wouldn't have the satisfaction of seeing her at the mercy of her emotions. *Look away*, she silently willed him.

He began to check his rifle. His attention diverted, she began to work the ropes against the bark once more. There was no way to protect her wrists, and blood welled from the scrapes she was inflicting. She kept on, feeling a slight give as a strand fell away. Or was it her desperate imagination? Ferris was almost finished inspecting his gun.

Vance would appear any moment around the slight bend in the trail near the tumbled pile of granite.

Picturing him walking into Ferris's sights made her work more feverishly. There would be no way Ferris could fail to shoot him dead, no way for Vance to even draw his revolver without being seen. Tears welled in her eyes from the pain in her wrists, but she kept on. Another strand. She had no gun, but she'd distract Ferris, dive at him, throw rocks, anything she could think of if only she could free herself.

Ferris picked up his binoculars and scanned the trail. "Like clockwork. Here comes the mighty Vance Silverton, meek as a kitten."

She needed more time. She sawed, frantic now. Another thread gave way. Her nerves knotted as she saw a shadow cross the path. *Vance...*

Warm blood seeped into her jacket cuffs as she scraped for all she was worth, the bark embedding itself into her wounds. *Please, God...please.*

Vance stepped partially into view. She couldn't see his expression, but she could imagine his resolve, the handsome cut of his jaw, the crow's feet around his eyes, the full mouth set in a determined line.

"If there's a gun in your hand, I shoot your girl," Ferris shouted.

Vance stopped, still cloaked in shadows. "No gun."

The rope came loose. She batted it away.

As she broke from the tree, a spark ignited in the darkness where Vance stood.

A flaming pine cone streaked through the air, thunking Ferris squarely on the side of the face.

His pinecone must have found its mark because he heard Ferris swear a moment before he began shooting. A bullet whistled past Vance's chin as he rolled to the side. He prayed Ferris kept his shots focused on him instead of Stephanie. He hopped to his feet and sprinted, gun in hand.

Ferris fired again but he was clearly still off balance from the tossed pinecone because the shots sprayed wildly. Vance charged and there was no other choice but to go full steam ahead. He did not know exactly where Stephanie was so he wouldn't return fire. Old-school. Head-on tackle.

But he didn't make it in time.

Ferris swung around, took aim. He braced for the feel of bullets carving through him but instead he heard a soft thump from in front as Ferris hit the dirt.

Stephanie had launched herself at Ferris, landing with her full weight on his back. Ferris lost his grip on the rifle.

Ferris had fury fueling him and Stephanie could not maintain her hold. Before Vance could make it there to assist her, Ferris shoved her off and darted into the trees.

Vance rushed to her, heart twisted with uncertainty and fear. "Steph, are you...? Did he...?" His prayers and questions got all tangled up in his mouth as he reached for her.

With his assistance, she got to her knees, wobbling until he brought her into his arms. He pulled her to him, reassuring himself she was alive. Unhurt. She clutched him back fiercely with a strength that filled him with joy. He relished the give of her soft shoulders, each shuddering breath as he held her steady. *Oh, Lord, thank You.* The words were wholly inadequate. He'd been near paralyzed at the thought of what he'd find at the campground, his only weapon a pinecone of all things.

She tensed and pushed him away.

"Get the dogs," she panted. "We can track him with his scent on the rifle."

He forced his brain to work. Ferris was on foot, without his rifle, though he had a handgun too. If there was any justice, he was stunned by the pinecone he'd taken to the cranium. Excellent. Too bad it didn't knock him out completely. With his jacket sleeve pulled over his fingertips, Vance lifted the rifle.

"Hurry," Steph urged. She was moving a step ahead of him, sprinting to the tent cabin, where the dogs were barking in frantic rhythm. They reached the door flap at almost the same moment. As she lifted her arm to open it, he saw the blood gleaming wetly.

He grabbed her and turned her to face him. "You're bleeding. What…?"

"Not shot. He tied me. I had to get the ropes loose."

He got only a glimpse of her ravaged skin before she pulled from his grasp and freed the dogs, who leaped all over her. Hot anger solidified in his gut, fueling his resolve as he held out the rifle while Steph clipped the leash on Chloe.

"Find," she said and he heard the emotion rippling through the word. Ferris had scared her. Hurt her. She would track him like the miserable fugitive he was and Vance would be with her every inch of the way until they got him or died trying.

She gasped in pain as Chloe tugged them into the night, Pudge staying by his shin. He yearned to take Chloe's lead and spare her the discomfort, but he didn't.

She wouldn't allow it and he wasn't skilled in handling a tracking dog. Instead, he focused on keeping Pudge close by and slashing away the branches that impeded their progress as they left the campground and entered the woods.

Ferris had a head start. He might be radioing his accomplice in the car to retrieve him. When he next clapped eyes on Evan, they were going to have a conversation that Evan wouldn't forget.

Intercept mode, Chloe, he urged. *You got this.*

Chloe did not slow for rocks or shrubs or anything as she bulldozed her way through the foliage. They were on Ferris's trail. No doubt about it.

"Close now," Steph whispered, struggling to control the dog. He detected the sound of the river, at first a murmur that rose into a shout as they barreled on. Ferris might be hoping to shake his pursuers off his scent by getting to the water but he'd underestimated Chloe. She was straining now, hauling Steph along toward the rocky lip that rose above the swirling waves.

"Wait," he called. Ferris was dangerous and growing more desperate and they were about to run right into him, he had no doubt.

He tried to stop her, grasping at her arm, but whether Steph's grip was weak due to her injuries or Chloe's animosity toward Ferris was unquenchable, the dog hurtled through the trees, emerging only feet away from Ferris. Uncharacteristically, Chloe barked.

Ferris reached for his pocket.

"Hands," Vance shouted, weapon drawn, as Steph attempted to quiet her dog.

Chloe growled and strained at the leash.

"Hands where I can see them, Ferris," Vance roared.

Ferris froze, considering. Then he lifted his palms.

Vance waited until Steph had Chloe quieted and her own gun out before he moved to Ferris and secured his hands behind his back, zip-tying them with one from Steph's supply. The satisfaction he felt at finally, finally capturing Ferris Grinder filled him to the brim.

He wasn't about to risk any further escape. Since they had no more zip ties, he settled for fastening Ferris's legs together with duct tape. "How's that feel, Ferris?" Vance asked. "Not too tight, I hope?"

Ferris didn't answer, his eyes glittering with hatred.

Vance removed the radio from Ferris's pocket, along with a satellite phone.

"Would you like to do the honors, Steph?"

Mouth trembling, she nodded. "I would."

He couldn't wait. She placed one call to the police with their location, a quick brief of the situation, and the second to Security Hounds, smiling as she waited for someone to pick up. After the agony they'd endured…it was about to be over.

Ferris looked up and heaved a deep

breath. Steph's call connected. She opened her mouth to speak. Chloe went stiff. Ferris lowered his head and charged right at Steph. The phone flew from her hand as Ferris crashed into her.

Vance shouted as Stephanie and Chloe were knocked into the swollen river.

FOURTEEN

Water struck Stephanie like a punch as she tumbled into it. The cold stripped her of breath as she went under, then she shot up, in shock from the frigid temperature. She twisted in a violent effort to keep from being sucked below again. Her clothes acted like a sponge, weighing her down.

"Chloe," she screamed, spray stinging her eyes.

To her left she saw an upturned paw, a glimpse of her bloodhound fighting as hard as she was. *Hang on, baby.*

She bobbed forward, struggling to snatch at any glimmer of wet fur, but the waves tossed her as if she was a load in the washing machine. Chloe appeared for a heart-stopping second, then disappeared. Steph paddled in a circle, an agonizing effort, but she could not spot her dog. She screamed again. A torrent of water rolled over, filling her mouth and nose. When she broke the surface, she gulped in a breath and tried to get her bearings. *Don't panic. Keep it together.* She was moving rapidly away from the point where Ferris had knocked her in, where Vance was probably out of his mind with worry.

Would she live to see him again?

The steep bank flashed by—exposed roots, swirling waves, a glimpse of rock. That was her greatest enemy as the surge propelled her along—being crushed against one of the boulders that poked up from the riverbed. One knock on the skull and she'd be dead. Chloe too.

"Chloe, talk," she hollered, after spitting out a mouthful of the river.

Was that a faint bark she heard? She thrashed in the opposite direction.

Chloe appeared a couple of feet away. "Chloe," she called but another wall of water inundated her, and when she was done sputtering and choking, she couldn't see Chloe anymore. She fought down the fear. *You're not going to drown, Chloe. I'm not going to let you.*

"Chloe, talk," she screamed again.

Another bark. Closer.

Chloe bobbed to the surface ten feet away, paddling hard.

She tried to swim for the dog, but she was thrown on her side, sucked under the freezing water. The cold was overwhelming, but she battled free once more. In the distance she saw the outline of a massive tree trunk spanning the chasm. It rose a couple of feet above the waterline. Would she be able to catch it? Hang on and haul herself to safety?

Not without Chloe. She wasn't going to leave her best friend to drown.

"Chloe," she yelled, narrowly avoiding being impaled by the sharp end of a branch. More branches appeared between the ripples. She hooked an arm around the next one she passed and was yanked to a halt so hard she bit her lip. It was a brutal effort to cling there with the river thundering around her, but she held on, praying the branch wouldn't break. She yelled again for Chloe to talk. *Answer me, Chloe. Please.*

The bark was louder now. Ears—she saw a glimpse of those incredible flappy ears.

"Come, Chloe. Come." Her heart quivered as Chloe surged toward her, powerful legs churning. The water fought against the dog, snatching her away until she fought back.

"You can do it." Her arm stretched out until her sinews almost snapped. "Come on. Come to me, girl. Please." The last word came out as a sob.

Snout low, Chloe steamed forward like a battleship.

"Almost there. Two more feet. Push hard."

She came close enough that Steph grabbed a strap on her harness and hauled her in.

Chloe looped those ridiculously long legs over Steph's shoulders and she and her dog clung close, hearts beating wildly. The wet fur against her cheek filled her with gratitude and renewed her determination. God gave her Chloe and they'd survive this. For a moment, maybe more, they held on to each other, stationary in the wild chaos. They could not remain that way for long. Steph's arms were trembling, Chloe's added weight making it harder to maintain their position. The branch she held shuddered ominously.

Next step. Should she let go? Hold on to Chloe and let the water carry them to the makeshift log bridge? Would she be able to snag hold and get them both out? She wasn't sure what lay beyond. A safe spot to wade out or a dangerous plunge or twist?

They couldn't remain with their body temperatures dropping, sucking away their strength. Vance would come, she was sure of it, but it would take time, more than they had. So it really wasn't a choice, was it?

She kissed Chloe. Their partnership was one of ultimate trust in one another. Whatever came, they'd endure it together. "No matter what, you are the best dog in the entire world, and I love you."

Chloe licked the moisture from Steph's face.

"All right. Hold on tight, sweet girl. Ready?"

With a fervent prayer and her pulse galloping, she let go.

Vance could barely contain his fury as he hauled Ferris away from the bank and tied him to the tree like he'd done with Evan. A furnace was burning inside him—Steph's shocked expression as she and Chloe went over was seared into his brain.

Ferris laughed. "Didn't get you, but at

least I got her and her dog. Two for two, which isn't bad. My daddy always taught me to maximize the wins where you can."

Rage curled his hand into a fist and he fought the urge to use it on Ferris, to smash the wicked grin from his mouth. The seconds ticked loudly in his brain, each one ripping Stephanie and Chloe farther away from him. He didn't trust himself to speak as he searched for Ferris's phone and radio while Pudge barked and whined at the edge of the river where Steph and Chloe had disappeared.

He found the radio, pocketed it and dialed the emergency number on the sat phone. When the sheriff's department answered, he launched in with the terrible update.

"This is Vance Silverton. You just got a call from Stephanie Wolfe, but the situation's changed. I've still got Ferris Grinder secured at…" He checked the coordinates and relayed them again. "But he's shoved Stephanie Wolfe and her dog into the river.

I'm going after them. Come get him and send help."

There was no need to whistle for Pudge. He was already slipping and sliding down the bank. As Vance followed, Ferris called out again.

"You're going to die too. If the river doesn't get you, I will, sooner or later, in a way you don't expect. Just know when you're dying, it was my doing."

Jaw clenched, he didn't answer, simply made his own ungainly way to join Pudge as he slid down the steep bank. They'd continue in the muddy margins as best they could, climb around obstacles when needed, follow the direction where Steph and Chloe had been carried.

He didn't feel the cold, the water droplets splashing at him, the mud oozing into his boots. All his emotion was funneled into one crystal-clear desire.

Find them.

But the freezing water was roaring, punishing the rocks and trees and anything it encountered. They had to make faster progress. He upped the pace, and Pudge maintained position at his side. When they encountered an enormous cleft in the bank, they scrambled to higher ground to skirt it, which cost them precious time.

Returning to their course along the river, he saw no sign of Steph or Chloe. He roared her name every few minutes and his heart sank lower when he received no replies. Had he and Pudge passed them somehow? Were they clinging to a rock or had they managed to pull themselves out and they'd rushed by the two? Worse thoughts threatened his sanity but he refused to give them purchase. *Keep going,* his instincts told him.

Another quarter mile, maybe a half, and he was feeling the tug of panic along with the burning in his legs. Doubt and fear overwhelmed him.

Lord, please.

Pudge dropped to his tummy, tongue lolling, but Vance could not stop. The next few yards might reveal Chloe and Steph. Pudge barked, but Vance rushed ahead, around the massive log that spanned the river. Something was nibbling at the edge of his consciousness, a change in the sound of the water. Vance's senses picked up on the information before his brain could.

Twenty yards past the fallen log, the riverbed plunged steeply, funneling into twisted rapids that pounded through a pinch point lined with sharp-edged rocks on either side. A death trap. His spirit dropped. The flow was raging with such force Steph and Chloe would not have been able to fight it. Unable to slow or stop, they would have been crushed against the rocks and been borne away.

He could not make himself believe it. It couldn't have ended that way. They must have gotten out somehow. Frantically he yanked the binoculars from his pack and scanned, praying for a glimpse of Steph or Chloe, safe on the bank.

There was no sign of either.

No Steph.

No faithful bloodhound.

It was as if the spirit drained out of him along with the last dregs of energy and hope.

He sank to his knees. Too late. He'd been too late.

If he hadn't stopped to call the police? Tie Ferris to the tree? What had he done? Had his desire to secure justice for Lettie caused him to sacrifice Steph? It was agony even to breathe in and out.

Pudge barked but he barely heard.

He couldn't absorb the enormity of what had happened. One moment, they'd been celebrating Ferris's capture, and then...

Pudge appeared at his elbow and barked again, whapping him on the shoulder with his snout.

Vance blinked, tried to focus. "What?"

Another bark. Another tap. Pudge about-faced and waddled rapidly upstream.

Upstream? Why there? The dog was definitely trying to tell him something.

But Pudge wasn't a tracker. Could this misfit dog, the oddball, untrained hound, know something about Stephanie and Chloe that he didn't? Pudge was a shipwreck in many ways, but the animal loved Chloe and Steph too, he had no doubt.

Should he follow Pudge or call the police again?

He clambered to his feet. "Pudge?"

The dog looked back once and let loose one loud, forceful come-here bark.

Vance summoned the strength to sprint after him. Pudge was panting, tongue lolling, when he finally heaved himself to a stop back at the spot of the fallen log. Vance used the binoculars and swept them over the span. There was nothing. Despair weighed him down.

"I don't see anything," he said to Pudge.

Pudge rose up on his back legs and head-butted Vance right in the stomach.

"I can't…"

As he straightened, he got a glimpse in the pocket of water contained by the roots of the fallen giant, a gleam, a soft shape where there shouldn't be any, the curve of an arm.

"Steph," he yelled.

She didn't answer, or maybe she simply didn't hear over the tumult. With Pudge at his side, he charged toward the tangled roots, his sight obscured by the water spraying into the darkness as they climbed up and over the mighty limb.

Pudge found them first, barking and panting, climbing and stumbling through the tangle of roots. Chloe's answering howl sent a shiver of pure joy right through him. But Steph. What was her condition?

He charged on, heedless of the roots grabbing for his ankles, hauling himself up and over piles of brush until he reached them.

Chloe sat on her haunches, shivering, her body leaning over Steph.

Steph was lying on her side in the fetal position, eyes closed.

Lord, oh, Lord, please... The words

repeated over and over in his soul as he dropped to his knees and touched her face—it was ice cold.

"Steph," he whispered, searching for a pulse on her neck. No thrum of life penetrated his frozen fingertips. "Open your eyes, honey. Please, please, please."

Had she stirred? Or was it his overwhelming need confusing him?

"Steph?"

Her mouth moved. Heart slamming, he pushed closer.

"What took you so long?" she whispered.

Joy swept him up in an intense wave as he bent over her, stroking the wet hair from her face, stripping off his jacket to cover her. "You scared me, Wolfe." He gently checked her limbs for obvious breaks.

"Nothing broken," Steph murmured. "How's Chloe?"

He spared a look. "Pudge is licking her

all over and she seems to be passing inspection. Can you sit up?"

She stirred.

"Slow, Steph. Take it easy. No rush, right?" But there was an urgency because she was undoubtedly becoming hypothermic. "Cops are alerted and on their way. Gotta get you warm in the meantime."

"Ferris?"

"Tied to a tree."

"Any way he could escape?"

"I'm gonna say no on that."

But Ferris's last comment echoed in his mind.

If the river doesn't get you, I will, sooner or later, in a way you don't expect.

His gut tightened. The river hadn't won and it wasn't going to. And neither was Ferris.

He bent and picked her up, her frame trembling with cold. "Chloe, are you okay to walk, girl?"

Chloe stood on shaky legs, Pudge nosing her with concern. Together, they picked their way over to a more sheltered spot, drier, farther from the roaring water. He set her down against a thick trunk and spread a silver emergency blanket from his pack, one for her and Chloe to sit on and the other to wrap around them over his jacket.

"You're cold and wet too," she said. "Take your jacket back."

He snorted. "As if. I'm a Marine, baby. We know stuff, we do things, and we never get cold." His goose bumps said otherwise, but he cheerfully ignored them. He gathered up as many dry leaves as he could find, as well as fallen bark, then piled everything up and coaxed out a flame with the waterproof matches from Steph's pack.

The blaze was tiny at first, but the way it danced life into her eyes gave him hope. More and more fuel he piled on until it was a sizable fire. It would help the rescuers find them.

"Can you feel it yet?"

She shook her head. "Not y-yet," she

said through chattering teeth. He sat next to her, drew her into his arms, as close to the flames as was safe. He added another metallic emergency blanket to their pile. Chloe burrowed in on one side of Steph and Pudge squirmed under the blanket on the other, crinkling the material.

Steph laughed weakly. "Now I'm feeling it."

And he was too.

Such feelings as only God could understand.

He embraced the woman and the dogs and breathed his thankful prayer into the frigid mountain air.

FIFTEEN

Search and rescue found them two hours later, along with a park ranger and two cops. Steph was still shivering, but not as violently, and Chloe appeared to be comfortable.

Ferris was in custody, the cops reported. Finally. Vance provided a quick briefing, including where they'd left Evan, though he'd obviously gotten free and helped Ferris with the campground ambush.

"The horse," Steph said. "Evan's horse needs to be collected."

"Later, Steph. Let them transport you on a stretcher," Vance said.

She shook her head. "No. We'll walk to the vehicle."

"But…" His face had been so ravaged

with fear when he'd carried her and Chloe out and it had struck a chord inside her that kept on sounding. Trauma, maybe, but she took his hand, gripping it tight as she stood. Pudge pranced next to Chloe, who'd been thoroughly dried, and both dogs had been given handfuls of treats from their rescuers.

"We heard from your sister. She's been trying to locate you," the cop said.

Steph sighed. "Radio her quick that we're okay, otherwise she'll have had a platoon of Wolfes en route."

The ranger looked up. "She called the competition planners after your hang-up and they reported that you'd tapped out, gone to a hotel. We'll contact her and provide the broad strokes of what happened."

She groaned. "All the while we were running for our lives, no one knew what was really going on." Ferris and his clever deceptions.

She and Vance and the dogs were loaded up into the vehicle and taken to the hospital, where they were checked over and more officers took their expanded statements. They even summoned a veterinarian to the hospital to tend to Chloe and Pudge.

"You've got some story to tell," the doctor said. "Amazing you survived."

She wouldn't have, except for the fact that Vance had been with her. She wanted more than anything to sleep for another few days, but she could not rest until her family knew the reality of her condition from her own mouth. They'd only gotten a bare bones report from the police. She dialed, and Kara and her mother answered on speakerphone.

"What happened? I want the whole story," her mother demanded. "Are you positive you aren't hurt? The cops didn't tell us nearly enough."

"You might want to sit down for this," she told them.

Kara didn't interrupt. Her mother, on the other hand, peppered her with questions until Steph promised again that she and Vance were unharmed, mostly, and they would be on their way to the ranch within the hour. She hoped Vance would agree with her plan.

"No. We'll come get you. Right now. I'll grab my keys..." her mom said.

"No need." Especially since her mom was still healing from back surgery. "I'm leaving as soon as possible. We'll be home tonight. You can track my phone via GPS if it will make you feel better."

"Okay, sis," Kara said and Steph heard the tears. "I'm so sorry I didn't suspect anything. I should have known when—"

"No way. This is nothing anyone could have foreseen. Stop that line of thinking, pronto."

"I agree," her mother said. "When you get here, we're going to have hot soup and bottomless coffee while you provide every last detail. I'm going to wait to call your brothers until after you give us the 411 or they'll all storm the castle."

She laughed. "All right. I'll message you when we leave."

Vance and Pudge showed up as she was ending the call. She'd been given a shower, which stung every scrape and cut, especially on her abraded wrists, and a set of hospital sweats and a T-shirt. Vance was dressed in his own borrowed gear, the pants slightly too short, his hair gleaming with moisture. Pudge had been wiped down like Chloe and looked much more presentable.

"What's the prognosis?" he said.

"Bandages and ointment and a few stitches. Lots of rest, blah, blah, recommended. You?"

"Similar but no stitches." He smiled at her. "Not to put too fine a point on it, but you look amazing for a woman who fell in the river."

"And you are pretty put-together too, considering you came after me."

"Steph—"

"I want to go home," she said, cutting

him off. The need was so great to return to the Security Hounds Ranch, she swallowed her pride. "Will you drive me? Now? My wrists hurt too bad to steer. We can rent a car. I know it's late in the day and a lot to ask, but…"

He was already pulling out his phone. "Wireless. I'll never take it for granted again. I'll get us a set of wheels right now. What do you want? A Corvette? Rolls?"

"Something that the dogs can slobber on." She laughed, feeling lighter than she had in years. More specifically, better than she'd been since Vance got the detective's job. She looked over at him.

"I'm on hold. What's the smile for?" he said.

"Just thinking about your cake."

"Oh, yeah." He looked suddenly shy. "You said… You said you'd come over and have chili when you delivered it. Is that still okay with you? Unless you've changed your mind since we're back in civilization."

Her insides quivered. What would happen between them now that they were back in the real world? The forgiveness was cemented, she knew, but she wasn't sure about their romantic status. He clearly wanted to start over. Did she? Could she? "Yes," she said faintly. "When things settle."

"When things settle," he repeated and the disappointment rang in his voice.

She felt suddenly nervous.

"Okay," he said. "I'll get us that car."

The trip was more uncomfortable than she'd imagined, but the pain reliever they'd supplied in the hospital took the edge off to the point that her eyelids had grown heavy. Her chin hit her chest twice as she struggled to stay awake. She forced herself straighter in the seat.

"Vance, there's something I can't figure out."

"I'm listening," he said around a mouthful of licorice. He'd been eating since they left the hospital and seemed to show no signs of stopping.

"How did Ferris find Evan when we had his phone and radio?"

"I wondered that myself. And further, why did he take your vehicle to try and capture us instead of whatever he'd rode in on?"

"Questions, more questions," she said sleepily, unable to stifle her yawn.

"Important thing is we made it out."

She yawned again.

He chuckled. "The details can wait. Go ahead and rest. I got this."

She dozed, swimming to consciousness hours later when they reached the gate that led to the ranch just before sundown. It was open and she smiled. Normally, every visitor would be greeted by a baying chorus of canines, but it was quiet since Roman, Garrett and Chase and their dogs were all elsewhere. Her mom's elderly bloodhound, Arthur, was likely lazing on the back lawn. Kara was tending a dog with medical issues who was finishing up a stay at the animal hospital.

Vance parked, got out and stretched, his groan echoing her own myriad of aches and pains. He clamped a hand to his back. "I am never sleeping on the ground again. Ever."

"Agreed."

Eager as she was to see her sister and mother, she got out of the car and took a moment to smooth her hair, straighten the borrowed clothes. Her family would be worried enough. The story would have to be told in pieces to cover everything they'd experienced. Multiple times, since her brothers would demand a thorough report too, when they returned home.

Where to start?

Vance shifted, eyeballing the house. His mouth twitched uneasily. Was that a sheen of perspiration on his brow? He caught her looking. "Uh, your family, your mom in particular, well, they weren't my biggest fans when I messed things up with you."

She laughed. "You scared of my mom?"

"One hundred percent," he replied solemnly.

"Not scared of my three brothers?"

"Nah, I can take them, but your mom…" He shook his head. "Whole other level of scary."

"Go on, Marine. Take your medicine like a big boy."

With a sigh, he saluted, squared his shoulders and pivoted to the house.

As she started to follow, her phone rang.

Vance was already striding to the door, his arms full of Pudge while Chloe waited at her side.

"Go on ahead," she called to Vance. "I need to take this. It's the cop from Lost Sierra."

Vance obliged and lugged Pudge along, only setting him on his feet on the front porch before he knocked politely.

"Hello, Officer," she said into the phone.

"Good afternoon, ma'am. You asked me to call you when we found the horse."

Evan's horse. She'd been concerned about the animal running loose without care. "Is he in good shape?"

"Yes, ma'am. He was standing pleased as punch right next to his owner, who was also in fine condition before we booked him."

"Wait. His owner?"

"Yes, Evan Bowman, the man hired by Ferris. He came clean about everything. He'll be an excellent witness when Ferris is tried."

The first flush of fear pricked her skin. "You found Evan Bowman tied to the tree."

There was a pause. "Yes. Right in the location you told us about when we debriefed."

Her body went cold. If Evan had been tied to the tree the whole time, who'd been driving the car when Ferris approached the campground? Her mind spun. Who would have been able to rendezvous with

Ferris? Someone who'd been in on the whole plan. But if not Evan...

"Ms. Wolfe?" The officer's voice came from far away. "Is everything okay?"

Her vision swam. Somebody who'd helped him lure her there, delivered her right to the spot where he was waiting to shoot. Her gaze caught tire tracks pressed into the mud on the side of the driveway marking the path a car had taken around the side of her home. Out of sight. "Dispatch local PD to this address," she said as she rattled off the location. "I..."

The words were swallowed up by a gunshot.

A second after the door swung open, the bullet pierced Vance's shoulder and exited the other side, spiraling him sideways into the doorframe before he hit the entry hall floor. Dazed, he didn't feel the pain as much as he experienced the shock. Blindsided, he found himself staring up at Gina, the woman he hadn't saved from the river. She stood with hands locked around a gun. Pudge howled in panic, dancing in frenzied uncertainty next to Vance.

Gina glared.

"Don't…" He'd started to call out a warning to Steph but it was too late—she was already there behind him, gripping her own weapon, advancing.

He managed to sit halfway up. Pudge pawed and barked while Chloe howled behind him at Steph's side. Try as he might, he couldn't get himself to his feet. His muscles simply wouldn't obey. The blood coursed a warm trail, soaking his sleeve, and he finally understood what had been bothering him since that moment at the Jeep. It was the look on Gina's face when he'd tried to save her from drowning in the creek. She hadn't been plucked from his grasp by the water. She'd *let go*. He'd disastrously miscalculated.

He tried to think over the pounding pain in his body. Pudge continued to bark at full volume and Steph said something, but he didn't catch it.

Gina was wearing different clothes than she had when he'd tried to rescue her, and there was an angry scratch on her neck, but it was her eyes that called the most attention—cold, filled with hate, her intention blazing. She was going to murder them. That much was clear. What had already happened to Steph's family? His gut went cold. Had she already killed them?

"Put your gun down," Gina said to Steph.

"That's not going to happen." Steph moved closer, Chloe next to her. "Where's my family?"

"I'll kill him," Gina said, pointing to Vance. "Shoot him right in the head."

"Police are already rolling." Steph stepped around him, advancing toward Gina. He tried to catch her attention, command her to stop.

But she kept her focus riveted on Gina. "Vance?" she said without looking at him.

"All fine here. A through-and-through." But the next one wouldn't be, and he was desperate to think of a plan to keep her from being Gina's next target.

"Where's my family?" Steph asked again, the urgency penetrating each syllable.

Gina laughed. "Awww. Are you worried? That's so sweet. But you deserve it, considering what you did to my family."

Steph tensed and he hurriedly spoke. "How'd you get out of the river? That water was frigid, moving fast." He surreptitiously snagged Pudge's collar with one hand, pulling the hysterical dog closer. Pudge whined and prodded Vance with his wet nose.

"I'm a good swimmer. I pulled myself out. Ferris was watching through binoculars and saw me fall in. He sent Evan to track me with the drone and pick me up. Evan set me up with a campsite and Ferris told me to wait there until he collected me."

"You were the one who drove Ferris to the campsite in my car," Steph said.

"Yeah. You were oblivious, both of you. After I dropped him in the trees and made sure you followed me, I drove to our prearranged rendezvous spot, left your car, and took off in Ferris's vehicle. He wanted me to get away clean and without being implicated." Her lips tightened. "But things clearly went wrong. He didn't show at the rendezvous. I hear he's been arrested."

Vance forced a chuckle. "If you ask me, things went exactly right. We left him all nice and trussed like a Christmas turkey for the cops to find. He sure wasn't happy about that turn of events. Grumble, grumble, grumble." Vance eased Pudge in front of him. "I take it you're the favorite cousin he mentioned. The one that had to leave town after he and Maurice were arrested?"

She glowered. He could feel Steph's tension as she aimed her gun. A standoff that would lead to death if he didn't do something.

"I had to move away," Gina snapped. "The police were all over everything, tearing apart the trucking business, making my life miserable even though I only helped with the computer work."

He watched her expression, bitter in such a young, delicate face. In other circumstances, she'd appear to be a complete innocent, a genial person whom you'd never suspect of such murderous tendencies. Another truth clicked home. It made sense now, why the Harlow family had opened the door to their assassin. They'd seen a small, harmless woman on the porch, not Ferris. "You killed the Harlows, didn't you?"

He heard Steph suck in a breath.

She shrugged. "They had it coming. And you do too. This was always our fall-back plan if something went wrong in the process of killing you two. First, we'd make Steph's family mourn, then your aunt Lettie. If Ferris couldn't complete the job, I would." Grim satisfaction rang in her words.

Steph spoke through gritted teeth. "Where is my family?"

"Locked in the basement, so I could make you watch while I killed them. Don't look so relieved. They'll die painfully too."

"None of this is going to help Ferris," Steph said. "He's on his way to prison."

Her chin went up. "Yes, it will. He'll know his father was avenged. I'll find a way to help him escape someday, but justice is the goal. It was from the beginning. Ferris says that's all you can strive for in this world."

Justice had been his primary goal too, for a while. And he'd allowed it to destroy things between him and Steph. No more.

"Gina," Steph said quietly. "This isn't…"

"Shut up."

Vance finally scooted Pudge into position. He used the dog's stocky frame to hide his actions as he reached to his waistband and palmed his gun. Pudge tensed and whined as Gina glared at Steph. "If you don't drop your weapon, I start shooting." Her fingers whitened on the trigger.

Before she could pull it, Vance let go of the dog. Pudge bolted, got his paws tangled and tumbled, his bulk sending him skidding across the floor. Vance and Steph both brought their weapons up simultaneously. Before Vance could get a shot off, Gina went over backward as Pudge rolled into her shins. Chloe raced to her friend's side and in the melee, Vance sprang on top of the pile and grabbed Gina's gun hand, pinning it to the floor. His shoulder was on fire, but he clung with everything in him until Steph pried Gina's gun out of her clawed fingers.

Vance flipped Gina over, ignoring the searing pain, and kneeled there until Steph found an extra leash to tie her hands. Pudge licked his face the whole time, and Vance put his good arm around his dog, who was whining at the blood pouring down Vance's arm.

"Good dog, Pudge," he said. "Best friend ever. I didn't know you were going to help in the takedown. I'm going to see to it you get a commendation for canine heroism and a piece of my carrot cake."

Gina secured, Steph turned to him. "Vance…" The pain in that one word. The fear. For him and for her family. His breath caught.

"I'm not critical," he said. "Go find them. I'll watch her."

He prayed with everything in him that she'd discover her family alive and unharmed. She raced to the basement door and unlocked it. Her cry of relief was overwhelming as he saw Kara and Beth Wolfe appear.

Thank You, God. His head spun with gratitude.

They hugged fiercely before the three hustled back to Vance again.

Gina remained tied and on her stomach. Pudge continued to whine and sniff at him, uninterested in the newcomers. Kara coaxed the dog a few inches away, her voice soft and soothing.

Beth took a knee at his side, assessing in the thorough manner he'd expect from an Air Force nurse.

"I sure didn't intend to meet you again this way, Captain," he said respectfully, using her Air Force rank. "I'd salute properly but…" But blood was pouring down his arm and he was beginning to feel lightheaded, his ears buzzing. *Do not pass out, Vance.* He closed his eyes for a moment and then refocused.

"Stay still," Beth Wolfe commanded. "Kara, bring me some towels."

Kara nodded, a phone pressed to her ear as she called 911 while Steph tied Gina's ankles. Gina continued to swear and scream but Chloe joined in with such an ear-splitting howl that Gina stopped.

Beth pressed towels to his wound, front and back. "Good thing you weren't standing two inches to the left or you'd be dead." He winced as she applied pressure. "Pain?"

"Hardly any, ma'am," he choked out.

"You are clearly lying."

"Yes, ma'am."

"Noted. And you're not going to give me some macho lip about denying a hospital transport, are you?"

"Wouldn't dream of it, ma'am." He squirmed. "Uh, but I'm making a mess on your hardwood. Maybe if I roll myself outside onto the porch..."

"Not necessary."

He shook his head. "Aunt Lettie spent years scrubbing floors so I can appreciate the problem. Bloodstains are a bear to remove. It'd be easier if I bled on the porch, ma'am, where there's a hose so you could..."

"Vance?"

"Yes, ma'am?"

"Stop talking."

"Yes, ma'am."

She smiled as she pressed the towels tight, which almost made him scream aloud. He ground his teeth together.

Beth regarded him, head cocked, mouth pinched. "Vance Silverton, you behaved like an imbecile and broke my daughter's heart."

He looked at her in mute agony.

The flared nostrils communicated her disgust along with the words. "I'd thought better of you, being a Marine and all."

That hurt. He wriggled, opened his mouth and closed it again.

"You may talk now," she said.

"I did behave dishonorably, ma'am. I treated her with disrespect. I am deeply ashamed of my actions."

Beth continued to work on his bullet wound. "She left the force because of you."

"Mom..." Steph said.

He looked Beth Wolfe square in the eyes. "Yes, ma'am, and I am truly sorry for it. Sorrier than I've ever been about anything else I've ever done in my whole life. If there was one thing I could do over, it'd be to change how I treated you daughter."

Beth remained silent for a moment. "You've told her so, I gather?"

Steph busied herself checking Gina's restraints. "Yes, Mom. He has."

"And you've accepted his apology, Steph?"

Steph blushed a cotton-candy pink. "Yes."

Yes. Oh, how grateful he was for that one syllable. Steph forgave him, but her mother was a different matter.

Beth patted Vance on his good shoulder. "All right. There's no need to discuss it further then, is there? Kara's called for an ambulance, and we'll save the soup and coffee for another night."

He nodded, dizziness overtaking him as Beth went to fetch more towels. Steph dropped to his side. "We make it through four days being hunted by a killer in the middle of nowhere and you get shot in my kitchen?"

"Front hallway to be exact." He smiled through the pain. "They say most injuries occur in the home."

She brought her face close to his and cupped his cheek. He stayed still, willing himself to memorize the feel of her touch, precious as sunshine, pure as a mountain morning.

"Hold on, Silverton." Then she kissed him hard, once, edged away and then again, softly, tenderly. "You just hold on, you hear?"

He wanted to reassure her, apologize again for the wound he'd inflicted, the mistakes he'd made, to tell her how she'd never really left his thoughts in the months they'd been apart, but he felt his stamina recede.

"Pudge..." he muttered.

"He can stay here with me," Kara said. "We'll take good care of him, I promise."

Pudge whined, pulled away from Kara and bustled to his side again.

The last thing he felt before he passed out was the tingle of Steph's kiss and the slippery slosh of Pudge's tongue on his wrist.

Steph looked with satisfaction at the message on her screen from the police department as she stroked Chloe's silky head where she sat next to Steph's chair. One full week after she and Vance had almost died in the Lost Sierra, justice was finally being served. Ferris was under arrest, as were Gina and Evan. The dogs had recovered fully and Vance had been stitched up and sent home. He'd already started house hunting for a rental that would accept dogs. In the meantime, he was bunking at his aunt Lettie's and Pudge was getting way too many treats from the woman.

Vance had called Steph every day and visited so often that her brother Chase had jokingly suggested Vance was the rea-

son he, Roman and Garrett were install-
ing a new security system. None of them
wanted to say out loud the real reason,
or to consider what might have happened
if Gina hadn't been stopped. She would
never forget seeing Vance lying bloody
on the floor, or the feeling of terror before she'd freed Kara and her mother in
the basement.

Kara looped an arm around Steph and
squeezed. "Okay, sis?"

"Yes." And she meant it. Nightmares
aside, her heart was at peace and her body
had almost fully healed, as had Vance.
God had blessed her richly.

"Good. Garrett said you're not to leave
the house without an escort."

"And Garrett knows full well that is a
ridiculous command which will not be
obeyed."

"Yep. He sure does." Kara snagged a bag
of carrots from the fridge.

"Hungry?"

"No, but the chickens are."

"I haven't forgotten about them. I'm still working on those plans for a more secure coop. Vance said he knows someone who might be able to help too."

"I didn't doubt it but hurry up if you can. I spotted two coyotes last night, licking their chops." Kara exited into the yard.

Chloe raised her nose in an alert a moment before the doorbell rang. Steph stuffed down a flicker of stress and strode to answer it, checking first through the peephole since her brothers hadn't yet finalized the security system. *You're safe. No more predators out gunning for you and Chloe.*

Her pulse bumped as she took in the tall, handsome man on her porch. She opened the door. Vance stood there holding a nervous Pudge. Pudge peered over Vance's arm, down at an enormous cream-colored mountain of a dog sitting attentively on the step. Pudge shot the large dog a look and scooted farther up toward Vance's shoulder as if he was trying to escape the jaws of a hungry tiger.

For a moment, her surprise left her speechless.

"Hi, Steph." Vance juggled his ungainly dog. "You're fine, Pudge. Absolutely safe. We talked about this, remember? Man up, would ya?"

Stephanie stared from Vance to the huge white dog and back again. "Whose dog is this?"

"Funny you should ask. Uh, remember when we spoke on the phone last night, I told you I knew a guy who could help with your sister's chicken problem?"

"Yes." She examined the dog closer. "Is that a...?"

"Anatolian shepherd, yes. Handsome, isn't he? He answers to the name of Phil. He was a livestock guardian on a farm, but it sold—you know, tough times for agriculture right? A real shame. Anyway they didn't want to take him along when they moved to the suburbs, so he landed on the unemployment line at the shelter with Pudge, go figure. He's the dog I mentioned Pudge was kind of afraid of, but Phil's not aggressive, just intense. You know. Kind of like you."

She blinked, trying to absorb it all. "Why did you bring him here?"

"Phil needs a job, and you need some chicken help, or at least, Kara does. Phil's got a whiz-bang résumé, though in his previous employment he specialized in sheep. Not a problem for him. He's versatile."

"Vance..." Words failed her.

Vance took a breath and kept going. "So, you know, I thought Phil could go to work protecting your sister's chickens. He wouldn't need to be doted on like Pudge here, because he's kind of an introvert, which is why no one seems to want to adopt him. A waste of talent, right? There Phil was in a cage, and there are your sister's chickens all juicy and vulnerable..."

A chuckle welled up from a spot deep inside and in a moment she was laughing so hard she was crying. Never had she seen a more adorable man. Pudge watched her and trembled. Phil was entirely unruffled by her mirth.

"I guess," she said when she could get a breath, "we could give him a trial run."

"Excellent. A probationary period, so Phil can demonstrate his skills." Vance eased Pudge down onto the opposite side of the porch step. The dog leaped through the doorway and cowered at Steph's legs. She reached down to pet him, still giggling. "Go sit yourself on the couch with Chloe, Pudge. She'll protect you."

Pudge scuttled off to join his bloodhound friend.

When she straightened, Vance was grinning. "This is terrific. We should totally celebrate Phil's new job."

"All right. What do you have in mind?"

"Is my cake ready? The carrot one with the rosettes and the tidbits?"

"Not yet."

He frowned, considering. "And my place

is all boxes so how about dinner out? We could talk about serious adulting stuff."

"Like what?"

He looked thoughtful, stroking Phil's neck in a distracted fashion. "My savings account and those plans."

"What plans?"

"The house plans. The property I bought is big enough for a three-bedroom place, two bathrooms, a yard for a garden and space for a bunch of dogs. I was considering putting in a video-game room or a home gym, but I'm not married to the idea or anything. As long as there's plenty of room for the two of us..."

She jerked. "The two of us?"

"And the dogs," he added quickly. "And a nice kitchen because I like to eat. You know I can take down a full side of beef in a week and however many carrot cakes are available. And a pantry for treats. That was Pudge's idea."

She put a palm on his chest. "Back it up, Silverton. Did you say the two of us?"

The moment stretched between them, full of a silent promise that made her heart thunder.

"Yes, I did," he said quietly, suddenly serious.

"That's going to require some explanation."

He encircled her wrist. "I meant you and me, Wolfe." A tentative smile broke over his face. "We go together like peanut butter and jelly, or ice cream and a spoon. You are the cheese to my macaroni."

"If you're making a joke..."

"I'm not," he said, applying pressure with his fingers. "Pay attention because I figure I'm only going to get one shot at this, you being the hard nut to crack and all." He locked eyes with her. "I love you, Steph. Like in that completely ridiculous, redonkadonk way that makes me want to wear socks that match and put money in a bank account and buy you roses every single time I pass the florist shop."

She gaped.

"Do you want me to list the reasons why? No problem. I came prepared." He released her wrist and pulled a rolled-up paper from his pocket. "I wrote it all down and Phil helped me edit. First, you are smarter and stronger than I am, even though my muscles are way bigger. Second, you sacrifice for other people, which is a godly quality if I ever heard of one. Third, I think you're beautiful." He looked up at her with a dopey expression as his gaze roved her face. "Like, you know, inexpressibly beautiful, from the inside to the outside, and when you smile at me it feels better than winning at basketball and that's something because I am really competitive and I win a lot. Fourth..." He squinted at the paper. "Well, I can't read my handwriting, but I think it's something to do with the fact that I never met anyone else in the whole world who impresses me like you do, and by impresses, what I mean is..." He waved a vague hand as he grasped for words.

"Vance," she finally said.

He stopped, and in that moment she saw through his genial facade how much he'd risked to profess his love, how deeply he cherished her and how precious this great big man was, with the dogs and plans and laughter and jokes.

Thank You, God. A lump rose in her throat. "I love you, too."

He pumped a fist. "I knew it." He turned in a circle and whooped to the sky. "Did you hear that, Phil? She loves me. I totally knew it."

Then he swept her into his arms and kissed her until she was breathless.

Three more kisses and they broke into laughter. Phil looked up at them patiently, as if waiting for their senses to return.

"You're hired, Phil," Steph said, still in Vance's arms. "Should we show him his new flock?"

"Yes, ma'am. No time like the present." But instead he kissed her again until she giggled.

"Are you sure Phil wants to come live at Security Hounds? It's chaotic here."

"Absolutely. He was born for it. Hop to, Phil," he said to the white mountain at his shin. "Me and the missus got to show you your new charges because we have things to do and plans to make."

So many things, and so many plans.

Thank You, God.

* * * * *

If you enjoyed this story
by Dana Mentink,
be sure to pick up the previous books
in the Security Hounds miniseries

Tracking the Truth
Fugitive Search

Available now from
Love Inspired Suspense!

Dear Reader,

There is just nothing better than a wilderness survival story, is there? Except maybe a wilderness survival story with dogs! Chloe is a champion bloodhound, but every hero, canine or otherwise, needs a sidekick, right? Pudge was a delight to create because he doesn't have an arsenal of skills, but he embodies the real qualities of a hero: faithfulness, loyalty, self-sacrifice and the ability to put himself in harm's way for those he loves. If he's out of shape, quirky and prone to fears of all kinds, so much the better.

There's an anonymous quote that says, "Home is where the dog runs to greet you." While we don't all have dogs, I hope that you feel the type of love that God has for you and experience comfort in your life, whether it's shown via the love of a dear pet, family members, or excellent friends. Thank you for joining me in this series adventure. Stay tuned for the next installment. I think you're really going to like the dogs you'll meet, as much as Pudge, Chloe and Phil.

Sincerely,
Dana Mentink